Human For Hire

Book 1

By

T.R. Harris

Collateral Damage Included

THC

Tom Harris Creations

Edited by
Lionel Dyck
Sherry Dixon
Grammarly
And of course...
Nikko, the Grammar Dog

Copyright 2022 by Tom Harris Creations, LLC

3 FREE BOOKS

No kidding. **3 FREE BOOKS**, simply for signing up for my email list.

Subscribe to My Email List
Go to bytrharris.com

Novels by T.R. Harris

<u>Human for Hire Series</u>
Human For Hire
Soldier of Fortune
Devil's Gate
Frontier Justice
Armies of the Sun
Sirius Cargo
Cellblock Orion
Starship Andromeda

<u>The Human Chronicles Legacy Series</u>
Raiders of the Shadow
War of Attrition
Secondary Protocol
Lifeforce
Battle Formation
Allied Command

<u>The Adam Cain Saga</u>
The Dead Worlds
Empires
Battle Plan
Galactic Vortex
Dark Energy
Universal Law
The Formation Code
The Quantum Enigma
Children of the Aris

<u>**The Human Chronicles Saga**</u>

The Fringe Worlds
Alien Assassin
The War of Pawns
The Tactics of Revenge
The Legend of Earth
Cain's Crusaders
The Apex Predator
A Galaxy to Conquer
The Masters of War
Prelude to War
The Unreachable Stars
When Earth Reigned Supreme
A Clash of Aliens
Battlelines
The Copernicus Deception
Scorched Earth
Alien Games
The Cain Legacy
The Andromeda Mission
Last Species Standing
Invasion Force
Force of Gravity
Mission Critical
The Lost Universe
The Immortal War
Destroyer of Worlds
Phantoms
Terminus Rising
The Last Aris

<u>**The Human Chronicles Box Set Series**</u>

Box Set #1 – Books 1-5 in the series
Box Set #2 – Books 6-10 in the series
Box Set #3 – Books 11-15 in the series
Box Set #4 – Books 16-20 in the series
Box Set #5—Books 21-25 in the series
Box Set #6—Books 26-29 in the series

<u>**REV Warriors Series**</u>
REV
REV: Renegades
REV: Rebirth
REV: Revolution
REV: Retribution
REV: Revelations
REV: Resolve
REV: Requiem
REV: Rebellion
REV: Resurrection
<u>*REV Warriors Box Set - Books 1-5*</u>

<u>**Jason King – Agent to the Stars Series**</u>
Jason King and the Unity Stone Affair
Jason King and the Mystery of the Galactic Lights

<u>**The Drone Wars Series**</u>
Day of the Drone

In collaboration with Co-Author George Wier...
The Liberation Series
Captains Malicious

*In a rough and tumble galaxy,
ruled by gun and muscle...*

*When you need the best mercenary, bounty hunter,
bodyguard or straight muscle,
you find a...*

HUMAN for HIRE

Chapter 1

"Is that him?" Kannin asked.

Axa pulled the curtain back so he could also look out the window. He shook his head.

"I do not know. He appears much too small ... and too young. This one is but a child."

Kannin grunted. "Looks are deceiving," he said. "Garis at the spaceport recognized the species, and he would know. He has been well beyond the Quadrant. He has seen them before."

Axa still wasn't convinced. He studied the slim creature walking along the far side of the street, looking for further clues as to his identity. The alien was barely over three-quarters the height of the average Anarean, slight of build and with pale, almost sickly-looking pink skin. His eyes were blue—yes, blue!—and he wore a tight-fitting cap with a wide brim on his head. A set of goggles were fitted around the cap, resting on the brim, telling Axa that the stranger came prepared for the frequent sandstorms on this part of Anarea. He was dressed in a tan-colored short sleeve shirt that was tucked into a pair of blue pants with pockets sewn mid-thigh, a strange location for pockets. Around his waist, he wore a holstered MK handgun, but Axa couldn't make out what model. He continued to shake his head, doubting if this was the creature everyone had been talking about for months.

"You know their reputation," Kannin was saying. "It would be wise to exercise caution."

"The stories could be myths," Axa countered, "self-created to instill fear and respect wherever they go."

Kannin laughed nervously. "It appears to be working, although I do not think they are myths. As you know, they once ruled the galaxy. That speaks to a particular set of skills few possess."

"Perhaps," said Axa, still not convinced. "But this thing is so, so tiny."

Kannin shrugged. "Whether he is the one or not, we should still inform Jorvis. It is what he pays us to do."

Axa nodded. "You are correct. I will tell him while you follow the alien. But not too close. You would not want to find out if the rumors are true about these creatures ... these creatures called *Humans*."

****

While Kannin set off to follow the Human, Axa slipped out the back of the building and hurried along the next street, dodging the transports as they hurried by. He entered another building where two Anareans seated at a table in the lobby instinctively went for their weapons. They relaxed when they recognized Axa. One of the sentries nodded upstairs.

Axa climbed the stairs and knocked on a door at the top of the landing.

"Come," said a voice from inside.

As Axa entered the room, he saw the gruff and solid figure of Jorvis Canara seated behind his desk. On the other side were three other creatures.

"What is it, Axa?"

"An alien has come to town."

Jorvis chuckled and waved a hand at his guests. They were all non-Anarean and of various species. "I should say you are correct. Please, my friends, forgive my associate. He has never been off Anarea."

Embarrassed, Axa nodded at the guests. "My apologies." Then he turned back to Jorvis. "Garis at the spaceport said this one is a *Human*."

Jorvis and his guests tensed.

"Is it the same one?" Jorvis asked.

"Unknown. He has only just arrived."

"Is the Human here to reclaim the credits?" asked a purple-skinned creature with ears that reached to his shoulders. "We invested much, making sure your operation on Zanor was successful. The credits are needed for the next phase of the operation."

Jorvis smiled and waved an impatient hand. "If this is indeed the same Human who has been going about the Quadrant apprehending people like me, then recovering any stolen credits would be one of his goals. However, my raids on neighboring Zanor have been going on for some time. They are a major source of funding for my syndicate. The recent theft on Zanor would be just another reason for the Zanoreans to hire an agent such as the Human."

Jorvis turned his attention to Axa. "Where is the alien now?"

"He is on Hallfin Street. Kannin is following."

"Then he will go to Yaffers; all visitors go there. Inform Constable Linnos as to the Human's arrival," Jorvis said to Axa. Then he turned and smiled again at his guests. "We will let the law on Anarea do to the Human what the law on Zanor cannot do to me. And then our visitor will find he has made a terrible mistake coming to *my* world. For on Anarea, there is no one more powerful than me. On Anarea, I am *The Human.*"

****

Adam Cain walked into the bar, temporarily blinded by the dim light inside. The place smelled of stale intoxicants and body odor, something one would expect on an arid world like Anarea. Through the gloom, he saw a dozen aliens—natives—all staring at him. This seemed as good a place as any to—

He suddenly saw stars and a moment later was tasting the bar's dusty and sandy wooden floor. As his mind quickly cleared, he recalled a split second before being hit as a boulder-sized fist slammed into the side of his head, coming at him from a darkened corner of the bar.

"They do not seem so tough!" bellowed a foul-smelling wall of flesh, even bigger than the average Anarean. The square-headed creature was leaning over Adam, his four-foot-long arms built like tree trunks and arched at his side as fists clenched and unclenched. "Humans! No match for Anareans."

Adam heard someone in the bar yell out. "He is but a child, Kronos. It is not a fair fight."

"Since when do Anareans fight fair?" the massive creature called Kronos bellowed again. Laughter erupted in the room.

Adam propped himself up on his left elbow while rubbing his swollen jaw with his right hand.

"I don't think I deserved that," he said to the towering Anarean. "I only came here looking for information. I am willing to pay for it."

"In Juirean credits, perhaps?" Kronos asked, pursing his thick lips. "We use JCs to make decorative ornaments for our females; they are so colorful ... and worthless in the Quadrant."

"Your females or the credits?" Adam couldn't stop himself from asking.

"Ha! The Human has humor in his soul."

"I also have energy credits."

"How much?"

"What do you know?"

"About what?"

"About Jorvis Canara."

Kronos grimaced as his massive head began to rock back and forth. "That, Human, was the wrong thing to say. Mistake me not, I will still take your energy credits, but now I will kill you first."

Adam let out a deep sigh while thinking, *Not again.*

In the blink of an eye, Adam lashed out with his right foot, sweeping the legs of the monster native. For such a tiny creature, Adam had more strength than expected. Kronos toppled over, hitting the floor just as Adam jumped to his feet. Then a powerful kick to the block head that would make an NFL field goal kicker envious was enough to put Kronos down for the count. But the fight wasn't over.

Adam turned to see two other Anareans with their weapons drawn. He almost laughed, seeing the panicked looks on their faces as they stood awkwardly waiting for the targeting computers in the MKs to find a lock in the dim light. They could have simply trusted their aim and pulled the trigger. But that wasn't what aliens did. Well, *most* aliens, but not all. Being an alien himself, Adam didn't subscribe to the traditional way of firing a handgun. He pulled his MK-17-Hybrid from its holster and sent two quick bolts center mass into the Anareans. Fortunately for them, the MK was set on Level-3, the stun setting. But still, it was enough to have an impact on the others in the bar. They'd never seen anyone draw and fire so fast—and so accurately—without relying on the weapon's targeting computer. Hands quickly pulled away from gun stocks, defusing the situation.

That was until Adam was struck in the back with another stun bolt.

For a Human, a Level-3 wasn't enough to stun them. But it was enough to knock Adam forward and back onto the floor. Then three more hulking Anareans were on his back, pressing gun barrels into his side and disarming him. He was rolled over, staring up at a uniformed native wearing a satisfied grin.

"I am Constable Linnos. I am the law in this town. I was informed that an alien with an attitude had arrived, one seeking to cause trouble." Linnos looked over at the still-unconscious Kronos and then at the two stunned natives near the bar. "I see the information was correct. You are under arrest, with charges to be tallied later."

Adam was jerked to his feet, lost in a sea of eight-foot-tall natives who pulled his arms behind him and attached corded metal handcuffs to his wrists. From past experience, Adam knew the cords would be unbreakable, but the connections were vulnerable. But this wasn't the time nor the place for a demonstration.

"He was asking about Jorvis," someone in the bar yelled out.

Linnos stepped closer. "So I suspected. You should know, alien, that Anareans look out for each other. There is no law in the Quadrant except what can be enforced, and foreign law has no standing here. If you violate the rights of a Citizen, then you will pay the consequences as deemed appropriate ... by me."

"I haven't done anything to *Citizen* Jorvis," Adam said in his defense.

"Ah, but you are wrong," Linnos said with exuberance. "On Anarea, even *contemplating* an offense is a crime."

"You can read minds?"

Linnos looked around at the carnage in the bar. "I do not have to. Any sane person can see that Humans are a menace to ... to everyone. Now take him away. And Human, you will find justice on Anarea is swift ... and final."

As Adam Cain was dragged from the bar, one thought kept rolling around in his head. *They don't pay me enough for this crap. Not even close.*

Chapter 2

After that, things went pretty much as expected. Adam was hauled into a police station not far from the bar and thrown into a cell with his hands still locked behind his back. He was hooked to a bar against the back wall as the three hulking deputies took turns pummeling him with their fists and alien bootjacks. It seems everyone had heard of the Humans, and the Anareans were anxious to test their muscle and brawn on the supposed superbeing.

Adam went along for the ride, moaning and groaning where appropriate, eventually feigning passing out, hanging limply from the wall. The guards unhooked him but left the handcuffs on. Adam collapsed to the floor, moaning as he did.

Constable Linnos ordered his deputies out of the cell and then locked the door, placing the electronic key in his pocket. He stood on the other side of the bars for a moment before leaving the observation room.

Adam climbed to his feet and sat on the end of the single cot in the cell. He was fairly beaten up, and blood oozed from his cut mouth. His body ached in a dozen places, even though that was changing rapidly. He surveyed his surroundings.

The Anareans were serious about their detainment facilities. The metal bars were solid and joined by horizontal members every ten inches, reinforcing the vertical rods. The alloy material would be strong, even as it was smelted to local standards. Adam already knew the gravity of Anarea was about three-quarters that of Earth—what was known throughout the galaxy as Juirean Standard. The steel wouldn't be as strong as it would be on Earth; even so, the way the cell was constructed would be problematic.

Next, he looked at the back wall. He tapped it with his elbow, surprised to hear the hollow resonance of sticks-and-brick construction. Most cells Adam had been in were made of concrete block, if not metal. He grinned, knowing there were locally grown wooden studs behind the wallboard of this cell.

Other than that, there was nothing else of interest in the cell or the observation area outside the room. All he had to do now was wait.

****

And he didn't have to wait long. Soon the Constable returned with another native which Adam recognized from the file he had back at his ship. It was Jorvis Canara.

The crime boss was larger than the average Anarean—more like Kronos than Linnos—with the customary block head and yellow eyes. He wore an expensive silken overcoat of simmering blue and a long white scarf flung backward from his shoulders, forming a cape. He had an amused grin on his face.

"So, this is a Human?" he asked Linnos rhetorically. "They are much smaller than I imagined." The native stepped up to the cell. "I am Jorvis Canara."

Adam remained seated.

"Yeah, I figured. You got here fast."

"My headquarters is not far from here."

"Then I was right."

"About the location of my headquarters? That you were. I operate out of the Tanus Fish Processing Center, but in reality, I control the entire city, indeed, the entire district."

"You smell like fish."

Jorvis recoiled and then laughed. "Yes, I do. You have a keen sense of smell."

"It's what we're known for."

Jorvis shook his head. "Not true, Human. Supposedly, you are a class of warriors rarely seen in the galaxy, much like the Juireans."

"We beat the Juireans," Adam said with a grin. "That makes us better than them."

"Ha, that is true," Jorvis roared. "I never liked the Juireans, and I have never met a Human before. But after the recent upheaval in the galaxy, both races are now mere sidenotes in history."

"With the Anareans destined to replace them?"

Jorvis laughed again, shaking his head. "My ambitions are much less grandiose. You can keep the galaxy; I will settle for the Quadrant."

Adam grimaced. "You do know it's not really a *Quadrant*? In fact, it's not more than a tenth of the galaxy, hell, not even that. More like a hundredth. But you can keep calling it *The Quadrant* if it makes you feel more important."

Jorvis frowned and Constable Linnos bristled.

"He does carry a certain reckless attitude about him," Jorvis said to Linnos.

"He is insane, that is what he is," said the police officer. "The arrogance of his race is evident. But he is living in the past. The Humans are nothing now, and with only a handful of them even left in the remains of the Expansion."

Jorvis shrugged. "That may be so, but this one has been causing quite the disruption within the *Quadrant*." He emphasized the word for Adam's benefit.

"He will no longer," Linnos pointed out ominously.

"That is also true." Jorvis leaned in closer to the bars. "My friend, the Constable, will soon pass judgment on you. He has that right. And what he will decree is what *I* tell him to decree. The mistake you made when coming here was to assume that not everyone in this part of Anarea was allied with me. They are. By coming here, you walked into the very center of my strength. Here, I am a world and you are but a person." Jorvis turned away abruptly. "But now I have guests I must return to." He looked at Linnos. "As entertaining as this event has been, I now grow weary. The Human is a disappointment. You may do with him as you wish. I will record this meeting as a revelation that the reputation of the mighty Humans is but a myth—a fantasy—and that any past glory they may have once enjoyed is long gone." He looked back at Adam. "I was so hoping for more of a challenge. Life grows boring when you sit atop the pinnacle, the master of all you survey."

Adam said nothing. Instead he simply winked.

The native frowned, not knowing how to take the gesture. It was not what he expected from a being about to be executed.

No, it wasn't. And that was because Adam Cain had no intention of being executed.

****

Linnos returned a little later, his face glum.

"I am in a quandary," he announced to his prisoner. Adam got up from the cot and walked to the bars, his hands still clasped behind his back. "Of course, I will kill you, or more correctly, I will *have* you killed. My problem is I do not want to waste the opportunity of killing a Human on some mundane method, one used on hundreds before you. I need to make your death an event."

Adam laughed. "So, you've come to me for advice? Sorry, I can't help you, except to say this. I'm not going to die here."

Linnos recoiled slightly. "You are not? Then that is news to me."

"It always is for my capturers."

"And why are you so confident that I will not kill you?"

"Consider, Constable Linnos, I have been operating in the Quadrant for six months and I have made nineteen apprehensions of fugitives or those sought by various private or government interests. Do you think that in all that time, only *you* and Jorvis have been able to catch me? Is your organization so much better than any of the others?"

"What is the point you are trying to make?" Linnos looked worried, even though he was on one side of the cell door and Adam was on the other.

"Ask yourself why I was so easily captured?"

"It was fortuitous. I came at you from behind. You were distracted by others in the bar."

Adam nodded. "That makes sense … if this were the first time I'd been in that situation. Honestly, I have been in similar situations hundreds of times throughout my life."

Linnos laughed. "Now I know you are lying. You are too young to have had so many experiences."

"I'm a lot older than I look."

"Which means what?"

"Never mind; it's not important at the moment."

"Are you telling me you intended to get arrested?"

Adam's face lit up. "Bingo … meaning you're right," Adam said before the translation bug screwed up the word *bingo*. "That's exactly it."

Behind his back, Adam worked the handcuffs, twisting them at the connecting joints between the clasps and the braided cord holding them together. The metal was bending...

Linnos shook his head, scoffing at the concept. "Then you truly are insane. Why would you do such a thing?"

"Simple. When I'm in here, and you're on the other side of the bars, you're a lot more willing to talk, to give me the information I need. And if your intention is to kill me, you'll tell me *everything*, thinking what harm could it cause? That's exactly what happened here. Jorvis came in and told me where to find his headquarters. I've been on-planet for about two hours and I already know where I have to go to get my bounty. Thank you very much for helping me, Constable."

Linnos waved his hand. "This is nonsense. Even if we gave you information, you have no way of acting on it."

"Then you won't mind telling me where my weapon and documents are that you took from me." He spoke loudly to disguise the subtle snap of the handcuffs.

Linnos was troubled by Adam's confident tone, but he wasn't about to give in now. "They are in my office," he stated defiantly. "Northwest corner. There, you now have more information which you cannot act upon."

Adam bowed his head slightly, resting his forehead on the metal bars of the cell. He whispered something that Linnos didn't hear clearly.

"What did you say?" He leaned in closer to the cell.

And that's when Adam reached out through the bars with his now-free left hand and grabbed Linnos by his thick neck. He pulled the huge block head against the bars, while bringing up his right hand holding a three-inch-long piece of connecting metal from the handcuffs he'd just broken. He pressed the rod against the Constable's neck.

"I said, 'Thanks. Now I can leave.'"

He jabbed the makeshift knife into the soft skin under the chin, grinding it in looking for one of the arteries that supplied blood to the brain. All Prime beings had such arteries, it was just a matter of finding it.

Blood gushed from the wound, bathing Adam in the red alien liquid. He spit when some of it entered his mouth. He held Linnos against the bars until the trembling body fell still, then he gently lowered him to the floor. Adam quickly rifled through the officer's pockets, searching for the keys to the cell. He put the control device in his pocket when he left with Jorvis.

But now it wasn't there. Adam panicked.

Then he looked across to a table set against the far wall of the observation room. A datapad was there ... along with a rectangular device about the size of a garage door opener. It was the key to the cell, and it was about twelve feet on the other side of the bars.

Shit! Adam thought. *Now what?*

He grasped one of the bars and braced his feet against another. Then he pulled with all his Human strength. As expected, the metal bent—slightly—but the reinforcing crossbars kept the opening from expanding enough to make a difference.

Adam spun around and looked at the back wall of the cell. He knew from the layout of the building that this was an exterior wall, with freedom on the other side.

He ran over and moved the cot away. He tapped gently so as to not attract the attention of the other officers in the building. He found a hollow area, and then using his body to help muffle the sound, slammed his elbow into the wall. The wallboard broke, a little. He hit it again, opening up a larger section that he could get his hands into. Desperately, Adam tore at the wall, pulling away larger and larger sections of wallboard until he had three of the vertical studs revealed.

On a light gravity world such as Anarea, cellulose material did not have to grow as tight and rigid as it would on a heavy gravity planet—like Earth. And with lighter loads to carry, the wood was lighter and more brittle, almost like balsa wood. Adam slipped his shoulder between two of the studs and pushed. He was rewarded when the boards split easily, opening a space large enough for him to crawl through.

Next, he had to get through the outer layer of the wall, and this was made of native brick. There was insulation to be pulled away before Adam could see the inner side of the exterior wall. He stepped back and placed a solid kick onto the surface. Nothing. Then a second kick, and a third. The mortar between the bricks began to crack and two more kicks was enough to open a space about a foot square. That was all it took. The weakened wall gave way when Adam stepped back and then crashed his body sideways into the barrier.

He tumbled out onto a concrete sidewalk lining a fairly busy road bordering the police station. A dozen Anareans noticed and stood gawking at the short alien who just crashed through the wall, now covered in red and white dust and lying on a pile of crumpled brick. If any realized he'd broken out of the police station, they didn't show it. Although they were surprised and possibly in shock, none of the eight-foot-tall natives seems scared. At six foot tall, Adam wasn't that imposing of a figure, appearing almost like a Hobbit to the natives.

Adam didn't waste time. He was free, but he wasn't ready to leave.

He sprinted around the side of the building to the entrance of the police station. When he was brought in he noted the location of the doors and the layout of the lobby. He also counted the police officers he saw. There weren't many, but he had no idea how many there were in the bullpen or the side offices. Still, he couldn't leave without his weapon, his ID, and most importantly, the keys to his spaceship.

Adam pressed open one side of the double doors and slipped inside, crouching to stay hidden in the visual shadow of the six-foot-tall counter that greeted visitors to the station. An officer was on the other side, working a data console and didn't notice the opening door. Beyond him was the bullpen where the rank-and-file police officers worked. Adam made it to the base of the counter and then slid to the side, looking around into the large room beyond. Two ... no, three other officers, two of which he recognized from the beating he'd taken earlier. This could be fun, getting a little payback.

Beyond the bullpen was a line of private offices for the senior personnel. The layout was eerily familiar to any number of municipal offices one would find on Earth. Prime beings—*Humanoid* to Humans—all had similar wants, needs and desires, which meant their buildings, clothing and mannerisms were universal, with only slight variations. It made working within the galaxy easier. Not easy, but easier.

Adam sized up the competition. Besides the native at the counter, there were three more in the bullpen, plus three others who appeared to be civilians. They didn't wear uniforms and were engrossed in their computer screens. Adam would deal with them if he had to. His goal was the large office at the northwest corner, the office of the captain of the precinct, or in this case, the Constable.

Adam moved back until he was directly below the officer on the other side of the counter. Then taking a deep breath, he crouched, firmed his muscles and jumped.

In the light gravity, Adam's Human muscles were enough to send him over six feet straight up and onto the top of the counter. The startled Anarean dropped his jaw and froze momentarily, long enough for Adam to take him out with a powerful kick to the chin. Then before the others in the bullpen could react, Adam braced his feet against the inner side of the counter and jumped, his arms outstretch like Superman, and directly into the back of the closest uniformed officer in the room.

He was seated at a desk, and the force of Adam's body slammed him into the desktop, fracturing ribs and collapsing his lungs. Adam was moving before the native gasped his last breath.

He was on the floor now, dodging between desks and closing fast on one of the officers who had beat him silly only half an hour before. Already, most of Adam's injuries were healed, including the cut on his lip. He'd let the Anareans believe he was hurt more than he was, having learned that acting defiant and semi-immune to such beatings only led to longer and more intense sessions.

His next target was also one of his attackers. The native saw him coming and went for his weapon. Adam recognized it as an MK-24, a mid-range model between the ubiquitous '17 and the more advanced '47. Adam had no idea what default setting it would be set at. But even at Level-2, although it wouldn't kill him, it would slow him down enough for the other officer to join in.

Adam threw his legs out in front and slid on the smooth, polished floor. He took out the legs of the much larger native, interrupting his aim. Even so, like most aliens, he would rely on the targeting computer—unless he panicked. Adam had seen that, too, where an alien started shooting indiscriminately. Alien aim was often atrocious, but sometimes they got lucky.

Adam and the native now tangled together, with the much smaller Human enmeshed in a forest of twenty-inch-thick arms. Fortunately, size didn't matter on a light gravity world; in fact, the lighter the gravity, the bigger—and weaker—the natives. Without the constant pull of heavy gravity, plants and animals tended to grow taller but less robust. Bone density was less, and flesh often softer. This was the case with the massive Anarean. Adam locked a Human arm around a matching native limb and pulled. A pronounced crack was heard as the police officer let out with an ear-piercing scream. He released Adam, more concerned with how his arm was now bent at a ninety-degree angle, and not at the elbow, than he was with the Human.

The next native lawman-like-thing had his weapon out and aimed at Adam. The light in the building was much brighter than in the bar, so the targeting computer would have no issue acquiring a target. The problem: It would take about half a second to lock-in at this range.

That was long enough for Adam to dive to his right to avoid the first plasma bolt. He slipped behind a desk, which would disrupt the computer, requiring another lock once the target was reacquired. Crawling on his hands and knees, Adam moved between desks, hearing the last surviving officer yelling to the clerical workers in the room to call for backup. Out the corner of his eye, Adam saw the civilians running for the exits, not wanting to get involved. Maybe once out of the room they would follow the orders. But for now, they didn't want any part of what was happening.

The officer was rushing between desks trying to get a bead on Adam. He fired again, this time without a target lock. He missed, but it told Adam he couldn't take any chances with this guy. He was either too scared or too angry to follow normal alien firing protocols.

Adam came upon a table instead of a desk, allowing him to slide underneath. He pushed off a desk and slid on the floor, coming up parallel to the mad officer a row of desks over. The native saw him, but not in time. Using his Human speed, Adam was up and across the dividing desk in a heartbeat. The two came together, a massive—but weak—creature against a smaller—but stronger and more dense—Human.

Adam grasped the thick wrist of the hand holding the MK. In turn, the Anarean grasped Adam's hand with his left and lifted both his arms—and Adam—high above him. Four-foot-long arms, combined with a standing height of eight feet, put Adam eleven feet in the air, taller than a basketball hoop. He dangled there as the native police officer fought to keep control of the weapon. He was yelling and growling, sounding more like a wild animal than a civilized Prime. He swung Adam around, sending his legs crashing into the sides of desks.

That's when Adam gave up trying to get the gun. His right hand was still locked around the native's wrist and unable to get free because of the second hand clamped around his. That still left Adam's left hand free. He flattened the palm and then sent his stiffened fingers into the throat of the alien police officer.

The impact was powerful and penetrated three inches into the flesh, making a profound impression on the towering native. Both his hands now moved to his crushed larynx, dropping the gun and forgetting about the diminutive alien he'd been fighting. Adam fell hard to the floor but was on his feet a moment later. The officer was now on his knees, writhing in pain and gasping for breath that refused to enter his lungs through his crushed windpipe. Adam recovered the MK, and feeling sorry for his victim, placed a bolt directly into his head. The ball of white-hot energy melted the brain, which then quickly expanded, causing the skull to explode. For the second time in half an hour, Adam was bathed in alien blood, but now with gooey grey matter in the mix.

Adam scanned the room. It was empty, although he heard a siren wailing from somewhere. His presence in the police station was no longer a secret and soon every officer in the area would be on their way.

Focusing on the corner office, Adam ran to it, bursting through the door. He looked around, finding his belongings sitting atop a cluttered wooden desk. With a sigh of relief, Adam scooped up his leather holster and wrapped it around his waist. He pulled out the hybrid weapon and checked the charge on the energy function.

When Adam began his new life as a gun for hire, he modified the standard Maris-Kliss handgun to include not only an energy aspect, but also a ballistic capacity, meaning he added a barrel, receiver and magazine holder for a nine-millimeter Human handgun. Bolt launchers were fine, if you had the battery capacity and weren't over a hundred yards away.

Adam preferred metal slugs to balls of energy, though both had their advantages. Ballistics could blast through barriers and had much longer range. But out here in the galaxy, finding a reliable ammo supply was the issue.

On the other hand, energy weapons could be recharged indefinitely. Their disadvantage: they had limited range, no penetrating power and limited capacity per charge. But the supply of charges was unlimited.

And that's why Adam decided to combine the two weapons systems into one deadly device. It was bulkier than either weapon alone, requiring modifications to his holster. But he liked the idea of having two weapons in one. And now, he wasn't about to leave the station without his customized handgun.

Next, he scooped up his ID and the keys to his starship. He laughed. *I wouldn't get too far without these*, he thought.

Even so, before Adam left the planet Anarea, he had a stop to make.

Chapter 3

Adam ran out through the front door of the police station, greeted by a gaggle of nervous and curious natives milling about, wondering what was happening inside the police station. The civilian workers had rushed out screaming, raising the alarm.

Adam looked around for a transport—a car—he could use. There was one half a block down, sitting at the curb with the driver's head silhouetted through the back window. With lightning quick speed, Adam ran to the vehicle and flung open the passenger side door. He fell inside the overly spacious interior—overly for a tiny Human; just right for a native Anarean. Adam placed the barrel of the MK against the forehead of the startled driver.

"Do you know where the Tanus Fish Processing Center is?" he growled at the native.

"What are you doing? This is my vehicle."

"Answer me, or you're going to *die* in your vehicle."

The native crossed his eyes, focusing on the barrel of the energy weapon still pressed against his forehead.

"Yes, yes, I know where it is."

"Get me there in one minute and you live. If not...."

"But it is five minutes away, maybe more."

"Okay, do it in two. Just get moving."

The driver turned his attention to the road. Most alien transports were controlled by a joystick setup on the left-hand side of the driver. Push the lever forward, the vehicle went forward ever faster. Pull it back and the car would slow. Then twist the crossbar to turn it left or right. It was pretty simple.

The native pulled away from the curb and merged with traffic.

"Only two minutes," Adam reminded him.

The car sped up and began weaving in and out of traffic, raising the ire of half a dozen fellow travelers.

"There is much traffic; I am doing all I can!" the panicking driver pleaded.

"Just get me there!"

Adam was watching out the back window. So far, no one was following. But he had to hurry. People like Jorvis had contingency plans for situations like this. Once word circulated about what happened at the police station, the gangster would be notified. Then he'd be in the wind.

They made it in two minutes, thirty-eight seconds. The driver, who had been watching a clock on the dashboard, was sure he was going to die. Instead, Adam shoved the gun in his ribs and told him to get out.

"But you said I could live if I got you here."

"And you will. But I'm taking your transport. Now, run, and don't come back."

The native obeyed.

Adam was out the door a moment later, his hybrid MK/Glock 9mm in his right hand, and the MK-17 from the police station in the other. The sign on the building was in Anarean so Adam had to take the driver's word for it that this was the place. It smelled like it.

Adam didn't bother with the door handle. Instead, he used his right leg as a battering ram and smashed the twelve-foot-tall panel into kindling. Two startled sentries tumbled out of their chairs at a round table in the lobby. They wore MKs. Neither had time to draw the handguns before Adam blasted them with Level-2 bolts from the police MK. But then the battery pack was drained. At Level-2, a standard charge only allowed for ten shots; the officer at the station had used up most of that firing at Adam.

A door at the top of the stairs slammed shut, giving Adam a target. He raced to the stairs and took the steps five at a time, reaching the landing two seconds later. He lowered a shoulder and crashed through the door before dropping to the floor and rolling.

A purple-skinned alien was in the center of the room holding a handgun. He didn't seem too confident with the weapon, but it didn't matter. Adam took him out with a bolt from his hybrid.

There were two other aliens in the room, but they backed away, holding their arms out to their sides. Jorvis wasn't among them.

There was another door in the room and Adam ran for it, again not bothering with the handle. The soft wood of Anarea made that possible. The moment the wood shattered Adam felt a burning sensation on his right chest. A young Anarean had just shot him with a flash bolt, but a Level-2. The force of the impact spun Adam around, which brought him back face-to-face with the shooter. Adam had his weapon ready and opted for a blast from the 9mm. The explosion was deafening, not something aliens were used to. They also weren't used to having a hollow point slug tear into their flesh center mass. At this range, and with the brittle bone structure of the natives, the bullet exited out the back ripping a four-inch-in-diameter hole in the already dead alien.

Adam didn't have time to savor the kill.

Jorvis Canara ducked through a doorway and out onto a balcony overlooking the street below. For a split second, Adam had a clear shot, but he hesitated. Fifty thousand credits ... dead. Seventy-five thousand ... alive.

Adam grimaced and holstered his weapon. Then he followed Jorvis out onto the balcony.

The gangster was waiting for him, carrying a three-foot-long sword that split at the tip like the tongue of a snake. Adam saw the glint of sunlight on the metal and ducked just in time to have the blade sweep by only inches above his head.

Jorvis was winding up for another strike when Adam ran forward in a crouch and tackled him at his midsection. The pair easily broke through the wooden railing and fell through the air, landing on the hood of a passing transport, with the huge native smashing down on

Adam's already injured chest. The driver of the car panicked and pushed the throttle, sending the fighters rolling over the windshield and then off the back of the vehicle. The road was made of a concrete-like material and was as hard as, well, concrete. Again, Jorvis ended up on top of the much smaller Human.

Having been cushioned by both falls, Jorvis was uninjured and began pommeling Adam with boulder-sized fists. Adam was coughing, trying to catch his breath and could barely block the punches as they came one after another. Jorvis had lost his sword in the fall off the balcony, so he reached for Adam's MK-Hybrid instead.

Seeing the gun, Adam reached out with both hands and took hold of Jorvis's wrist. The big Anarean tried to cock the weapon so it aimed at Adam's head but he had trouble with the added weight. Adam's senses cleared and his breathing stabilized enough for him to realize what he had to do. He squeezed the wrist of the native and pushed the gun away from his head, forcing Jorvis's hand to bend back more than it should. Like the officer at the police station, Jorvis let out an ear-piercing scream when his wrist broke. He dropped the weapon and held the limp wrist in his left hand, whimpering, looking at Adam with tear filled eyes and then at his useless appendage.

"You! You will die for this!" Jorvis spit through clenched teeth and quivering lips.

"Not before you do," Adam said calmly. He recovered his weapon and then stood up. They were in the middle of the street with traffic stopped in both directions. A hundred or more Anareans stood gawking, not knowing what to make of what they were seeing. A tiny, Hobbit-like creature had just bested their most famous resident. And he had a weapon. No one made a move to challenge Adam.

Even so, he had to hurry. The ubiquitous police sirens were growing louder and seemed to be coming from all directions. He reached down and grabbed Jovis by his shiny blue shirt.

The native slapped at his hand, still wailing from the pain in his right wrist. He tried to crawl away. Adam had had enough. He couldn't deal with an uncooperative fugitive. Stepping forward, Adam laid a sharp backhand across Jorvis's face, being careful to moderate the power so as to not kill the crime lord. But it was strong enough to knock him out.

Next, Adam took the long arms of the native and draped them over his shoulders from behind, before dragging the eight-foot-long beast to the transport he'd appropriated earlier. He opened the passenger door and shoved Jorvis inside. Then he went to the driver's side and climbed in.

For once, Adam was glad the drive controls were in a joystick to his left and not on the floor. If the Anareans used gas peddles and brakes, his legs wouldn't have been long enough to reach them. As it was, Adam could barely see over the dashboard to drive. He shoved the control stick forward and the car shot off away from the curb.

Working the joystick, Adam weaved between alien cars and trucks, watching through the rearview camera as a pair of identical grey cars followed him through the maze of traffic. These would be police cars, and they were closing.

Using the stick, Adam swerved left and right, slamming into other cars, causing them to lose control and spin in the middle of the street. Chain reaction crashes followed, and seconds later, the street, coming and going, was blocked. The grey police cars were on the other side of the carnage.

But that wouldn't stop them for long, and there were more on the way.

Adam knew how to get to the spaceport from here. He'd done his homework, studying the maps as he planned the operation. Sure, it wasn't so much a formal plan as a general outline. He'd been on so many missions like this before that he could do it in his sleep. But exfil was one of his main concerns, a concept drilled into him decades ago back on Earth during his Navy SEAL training. Not much mattered if you couldn't make a clean getaway.

Fortunately, the spaceport was only a few miles outside the city limits. Adam sped past lighter traffic on the main thoroughfare and was at the facility less than ten minutes later.

But the police were already there. A single car was blocking the entrance to the port, lights flashing along a strip that outlined the top of the vehicle. Two uniformed officers were on the other side of the car, aiming Xan-fi flash rifles at Adam's approaching transport.

Adam didn't slow down, but as he got closer, he spun the joystick steering bar all the way to the right, putting the car into a spin. He corrected when the tail end was facing the broadside of the police car. Then he pulled back on the stick, sending the transport into reverse.

He rammed the police car at about thirty miles per hour—or its equivalent in Anarean measurement—deforming the passenger side and shoving the car back into the police officers. They flew through the air and hit hard on the concrete road.

Adam didn't wait to check their condition. He shoved the control stick forward and spun away. His transport still ran, but barely. The back was smashed and the frame bent sideways making it hard for Adam to steer. Fortunately, most electric vehicles had motors on each wheel and although one wasn't working, it didn't lock up, allowing the tire to spin freely.

The next barrier was the interior security gate separating the service facilities from the vast landing and takeoff field. It was a thin arm blocking the road and anchored by a guard shack. The guard was outside his hut, looking toward the front entrance of the port, wondering what all the noise and commotion was about. He watched as Adam's smoking vehicle closed on his position and moved out of the way a split second before Adam crashed through the gate.

He raced off across the compacted dirt landing field, following a row of ten-foot-high markers indicating landing zones. The field was about half full, with a few ships on landing approach while a couple raced for the heavens on plumes of grey-white chemical jets.

His ship was in spot something-something 98. He didn't bother learning the Anarean color or symbol indicators, only the number. But as he grew closer to number 98, he started noticing something didn't look right. He slowed, checking the markers. Then he came to a stop, slumping his shoulders and sighing.

His ship wasn't there. The space was empty.

He stepped out of the car and did a three-sixty, scanning the field for anything that looked like his ship. It had only been three hours. He knew where he parked her and there was no reason for the ground crew to move the vessel.

A field service worker was about fifty yards away, sitting in a golfcart-like vehicle with a large trash bin on the back. Adam sprinted over.

"The ship in number 98, what happened to it?"

The droopy-eyed native looked at the spot.

"It is not here."

"That I know. Where did it go?"

The maintenance tech looked up and pointed. "It lifted."

"Who took it?"

"I do not know. I would say the owners took it."

"*I'm* the owner."

The native looked genuinely surprised. "Then it appears your ship has been stolen. Perhaps you should link to Constable Linnos."

The native didn't seemed fazed by Adam's blood-soaked shirt with the perfect circle burned into the right of his chest, the result of the Level-2 bolt. Adam didn't have the heart to tell the worker that some of the blood was that of Constable Linnos.

But now Adam had a major problem. He was about a mile into the spaceport and with no ship to get off-world, and with a couple of dozen angry eight-foot-tall police officers racing to get to him.

Adam shrugged. The solution was simple. He needed to steal a ship.

He looked around. About a hundred yards away was an FS-class muleship. The cargo string wasn't nearby, so either it had already been taken away or had been left in orbit. The vessel was a two-person model and one of the crew was ferrying five-gallon-sized metal containers in the ship through a side airlock. Adam recognized the species as Nosamin, basically harmless creatures who preferred making money to making war.

Adam returned to the smashed transport and hauled the still unconscious Jorvis Canara out of the passenger seat. Using only one arm draped over his shoulder this time, Adam dragged the gangster toward the muleship.

Along the way, Adam used his free hand to take out the MK-Hybrid and dial the intensity back down to stun. When he was about twenty yards from the working Nosamin, the alien noticed him and stopped what he was doing. He opened his mouth to say something but Adam shot him instead.

Without breaking stride, Adam dragged Jorvis through the opened airlock door, through the pressure chamber and past the open inner lock. He turned toward the cockpit, still dragging the native behind him.

The second Nosamin heard the commotion and had stood up from the pilot seat.

"What are—"

Adam shot him where he stood.

He spun the co-pilot seat around and set the huge native in it. Next, Adam fastened the seatbelt around Jorvis, making sure the shoulder and waist straps were secure. Then he took the center buckle in his hands and squeezed, deforming the soft metal and making the clasp inoperative, locking Jorvis in the seat.

Next, Adam took the stunned and unconscious pilot by the shirt and dragged him from the ship, grabbing his partner as he passed through the airlock door. He took them fifty yards away, clear of the blast zone before unceremoniously dropping the limp bodies on the dirt.

Adam returned to the muleship.

Flight controls for most FTL ships in the galaxy are all about the same, making flying a variety of craft a piece of cake. The muleship was no different. Adam slipped into the pilot seat, buckled in and then set about priming the chemical liftoff jets. At the same time, he started the gravity generator. It would take a minute or two to warm up.

Once the pressure in the chemical tanks was in the green, Adam pressed the ignite button and the ship rose from the surface riding a cloud of grey smoke. A muleship is fairly large and powerful, designed to haul long strings of cargo across thousands of light-years. Even so, they were lumbering vehicles within an atmosphere. It would take a full fifteen minutes to reach safe well-distance, the point where he could engage a gravity-well without it affecting anything around it, including the surface of the planet. Adam wasn't sure if he wanted to wait that long.

As soon as he lifted, traffic control was screaming at him on a link. He didn't have permission to lift and there were approaching vessels in the area. Coordinates were shouted at him which Adam quickly ignored.

In another time, disobeying spaceport rules would have gotten you banned from spaceports and whole planets. Not anymore. There was no coordination between worlds, especially in the Quadrant. You were more or less able to do anything you could get away with, and Adam was departing controlled airspace without permission or a flight plan.

Just then, a shadow swept across the forward viewport and the proximity alert siren sounded. Adam brought the topside camera online, seeing a massive plate of metal directly above him and with a dozen fiery jets outlining the frame. It was a major transport cruiser, one of the biggest ships that could land on the surface of a planet, and it was directly above him and descending.

Adam cranked the controls over, diving once again for the surface. The shadow seemed to follow him as the features on the underside of the cruiser became clearer ... and closer. Adam throttled the controls, angling the lifting jets more horizontal rather than vertical, sending the muleship racing parallel to the surface, but at an angle that was definitely headed down.

At the last minute, the muleship cleared the massive hull of the cruiser and shot off over the brown and arid surface of Anarea. Adam was well clear of the spaceport by now and out of the jurisdiction of traffic control. He checked the altimeter. He was seventeen miles up and with no other air- or spacecraft around.

Adam engaged the gravity drive.

Instantly, the muleship was within the event horizon of a microscopically small singularity, one created by the dynamo effect of the gravity generators and positioned according to the alignment of the mass beam by the focusing rings. Once in the gravity-well of the miniature black hole, the muleship *fell* toward the source, but only for a fraction of a second until the singularity dissolved and was replaced with another a little farther along the flightpath. Millions of such singularities formed, always at the same distance from the focusing rings, causing the vessel to continually fall toward an ever-moving point in space.

Within seconds, the massive muleship was in space and *falling* even faster as Adam cranked up the well intensity. Soon the ship was moving at many multiples the speed of light, safely ensconced in a series of event horizons that protected the ship and her occupants from the laws of normal space, namely time dilation and mass gain. Because the vessel didn't require energy to push it to ever higher velocities, it acquired no additional mass. The ship was detectible by modern tracking equipment, but it was invisible to an outside observer, hidden by the event horizon of the singularity.

At this rate, the muleship would be clear of the Anarean system in less than thirty minutes, and beyond the jurisdiction of local law enforcement. Of course, the forces on Anarea were free to do anything they wanted in open space, just as Adam could. They could chase him all the way to Zanor if they wanted. But the muleship was extremely fast when not towing a string. Adam could stay ahead of any active pursuit if the Anareans considered Jorvis important enough. So far, no one was following.

Adam steered above the plane of the ecliptic, making it easier to avoid any large-mass objects that could interfere with the gravity drive, and once beyond the system's Ort Cloud, he relaxed.

He looked over at Jorvis, who was groggily awakening. He had his bounty, although the success came with caveats. He was missing his ship, the ship that was his home. It contained everything he owned and cherished. All he could think about at the moment was how to get her back.

Adam worked the Continuous Wormhole communication system, creating a link with his boss, the Juirean, Tidus Na Nolan.

****

The pale, green-skinned alien appeared on the comm screen a few moments later. Adam didn't think what time it was on Tel'oran; Tidus had an apartment at the headquarters of his company, Starfire Security, and he rarely left the building. He worked when work was to be done, which was something Adam admired about the Juirean.

Tidus was awake, dressed and sitting at his desk. He looked down at a timepiece on the desk and grinned.

"Four hours, that has to be a record. I take it you had no problem finding Canara?"

"A little, but nothing I couldn't handle. Listen, I need you to activate the tracker on my ship."

Tidus leaned back in his chair and laughed. "Did you lose the *Arieel* again?"

"It was stolen this time."

"In four hours?"

"Just activate the tracker, will you? It's off planet, but they aren't that far ahead of me."

Tidus shrugged and worked his computer. Every ship had—or should have—a transponder code that was not to be tampered with. It identified the vessel to law enforcement and ground control on thousands of worlds. Most pirates knew how to disable the transponder or replace them with substitutes. Adam's ship had an extra layer of security, one that was undetectable to would-be thieves. It only became active when requested from Starfire after which it embedded the signal within the myriad of other circuits aboard the ship. Even if the transponder was disabled, Adam's tracker could still locate the ship.

"Okay, I got it," Tidus reported. "Let me check the overlay. It's making a beeline for some shithole called Ryndon. It's rated a three on the technology scale."

Adam always marveled at how Human-like Tidus spoke. Years ago, he had been one of only a few renegades to leave the Authority for a life beyond the rigid structure of his native society and its management of the Juirean Expansion. Tidus began working for Priority Acquisitions, the largest fugitive recovery and mercenary agency in the galaxy, spending years in the slums and barrios of a hundred worlds. He acquired the slang and mannerisms of dozens of species, including Humans. And now around Adam, he spoke and acted just like a wiseguy from New Jersey, but without the accent.

Adam worked the nav controls and brought Ryndon up on his screen. He checked the relative distances.

"Shit, it's the opposite direction from Zanor."

"I didn't ask, but is Canara dead or alive?"

"Alive; that's him moaning next to me. Hold on a second."

Jorvis was coming to, screaming from the pain in his wrist and as mad as a hornet.

"I am going to tear you apart and feast on your innards, Human! Record my promise. I will—"

Adam backhanded the alien again, knocking him unconscious for a second time.

"Okay, I'm back. You were saying?"

"Take him to Zanor first; it's only about seven hours away from Anarea."

"And Ryndon is twelve hours from Zanor. I may not have much of a ship left after that."

"I'll have people waiting at the spaceport to take Canara. You won't be there for more than a few minutes."

Adam slumped in his chair. That was one of the worst things about space travel, the hurry-up-and-wait aspect. You couldn't get anywhere in a hurry. After a mad dash to exfil from an operation, you spent days, weeks and even months twiddling your thumbs on the trip back to headquarters. It was an incredible waste of time and boring as hell.

It also came with the territory.

"Fine, I'll go to Zanor first. But if my ship is stripped by the time I get to Ryndon, I'm going to expect a sizable bonus on this job."

"A bonus?" Tidus exclaimed. "Hey, I didn't steal your ship. Maybe you should have locked the door when you left."

"I did!"

Or at least I think I did, Adam thought. He wasn't sure.

Chapter 4

Good to his word, Tidus had an enthusiastic delegation of anxious Zanoreans waiting at the spaceport when Adam arrived. Jorvis was just coming out of his third backhand-induced nap and his brain wasn't functioning quite right. He had no idea where he was. It didn't matter, the Zanoreans were ecstatic about getting their tiny, three-fingered claws on their public enemy number one. As they showered Adam with praise, he nodded and shooed them away from the muleship. He had to go, and anyone within the blast zone would be toast.

Adam cranked the gravity drive up to maximum, redlining the huge generators beyond safe operational levels. Legally—when there were laws in the galaxy—speeds such as this were reserved for the major space lanes where mass objects were few and far between. But between ordinary star systems, Adam was taking a risk. Space may appear empty, but in fact it was full of all kinds of crap, mass sources that could disrupt his well, or that could be sent off into wild and erratic orbits that could be a danger to other traffic or even neighboring worlds.

Adam didn't give a damn. Even though he made it to Ryndon in ten hours and twenty minutes, that was still plenty of time for experienced thieves to strip his ship bare. He'd never been much into sentimentality, but he had some neat shit aboard his ship, irreplaceable shit. Hopefully, the thieves would go for the electronics and other components first and leave his personal belongings for last. Either way, Adam was mad as a spitting viper when he entered the system and had to slow down.

"This is Ryndon Control," said the four-eyed being on the screen. "Controller Hasson Kri serving. State your intentions."

"I need a vector to the Issis Spaceport."

The alien looked at his screen. "That can be done, however, according to the transponder code for your vessel, there is a report that the ship has been stolen."

Adam looked at the creature and shrugged. "Yeah, so what?"

The alien shrugged back. "It is only for disclosure purposes that I inform you should any inspections or modifications to the vessel be required prior to or during your stay on Ryndon, it will be *your* responsibility as the possessing party."

"Yeah, I get it. How much to land?"

"Two hundred four credits for each segment."

"Each?"

"Landing and departure."

Adam shook his head. "I won't be leaving in this ship."

"Then you will need a residency visa good for one Ryndon year. That will cost two thousand energy credits."

"I'm not staying, only the ship."

"Then there will be a charge for storage until the ship is claimed by the next responsible party."

"How much is that?"

"Ninety-one credits."

"Fine," Adam said, exasperated. He just wanted to get to the surface.

"Please scan your payment chit for two hundred ninety-five credits."

After the charge went through, Adam was sent the vector coordinates for the spaceport. During the intervening seventeen-plus hours since Adam left Anarea, Tidus kept track of the location of his ship in case it bypassed Ryndon or left the planet early. It was still here, and had only arrived two hours before, having taken a more leisurely journey to Ryndon than did Adam. This only made Adam more angry, imagining aliens taking their time rifling through his drawers and storage cabinets, playing with his stuff.

When he finally landed, he was out of the airlock before the landing exhaust cleared. Ryndon had a thinner atmosphere than Earth, so he wore a light breathing mask over his mouth and nose. He had his MK-Hybrid secured to his hip and thigh, the flash component fully charged, and a fresh fifteen-round magazine in the Glock.

With a datapad in his hand showing the location of the tracking beacon, Adam set off across the grounds and through a forest of parked starships. As with all spaceports, this one was spread out and not much more than a large, dusty field. Some of the fancier ports had tarmac covering the surface, which required constant upkeep and replacement as take-offs and landings were hot and violent events. It was cheaper just to use plain old dirt, as ninety percent of spaceports did.

But that made for a lot of dust filling the air. Fortunately, the breathing mask helped with that.

The beacon was about a mile away and Adam set off at a fast jog, which on Ryndon would have set a world record for the mile run. Adam didn't care if he made a scene. He wanted to get to his ship as quickly as possible.

And there it was.

He'd christened her the *Arieel*, after his former girlfriend, Arieel Bol of the planet Formil. Arieel was a stunning alien beauty and the improbable mother of his second child, Lila, seeing that she resulted from an interspecies mating that everyone said was impossible. Adam's first daughter, Cassie—and her mother, Maria—died on Earth over thirty years ago during the Juirean bombardment of the planet. Although he worked for a Juirean and considered Tidus a friend, for the bulk of the Juirean race, Adam still held a burning, unforgivable hatred that was hard to hide.

The *Arieel* was a sleek, Borkin-class liner; a four-passenger model with dual Ronex gravity generators and Bimor focusing rings. The ship came with standard plasma defensive weapons, to which Adam added another set of turrets and a Browning Automatic Repeater zip gun from Earth. The BAR was capable of filling the space around the ship with thousands of deadly projectiles that could pass through defensive shields designed to stop flash cannon bolts, but not solid objects. So far, he hadn't needed any of the weapons, not since he bought the ship three years before. Of course, *bought* wasn't the right word. At the time, Adam was helping Tidus setup his new security company, so the ship was technically part of the business inventory. But everyone knew the *Arieel* was Adam's baby, what there would be left of her if he didn't stop the thieves from violating his starship.

Adam had his hybrid out, and although it went against his grain, the setting on the energy component was at Level-3.

Five aliens were working the ship, all of different species, and hauling metal boxes out of the airlock. A flatbed transport sat nearby, already loaded with a stack of boxes and other loose items. Adam's anger level soared when he realized the aliens weren't removing ship components but his personal belongings.

He approached without hesitation and sent stun bolts center mass into three of the thieves. Then he sent another into the arm of a fourth before striding up to the fifth thief and placing the barrel of the weapon at eye level for the alien.

"You better not have broken any of my shit," Adam growled.

Even though the green-skinned creature was intimidated by the gun in his face, he still managed to blink several times when the translation bug gave the literal equivalent for the word *shit* in his native language. In that context, the sentence didn't make sense.

"I ... I would not have broken your *shit* ... if that is even possible."

Adam shrugged off the comment. "This is *my* ship, asshole! Why did you take it from Anarea?"

"*Your* ship!" The alien seemed genuinely shocked. "Garis said the former owner would not need it any longer. That is what he told us. He said you were in some trouble in town and would not be leaving—ever. We gave him a fair price for the vessel. "

"Well, sorry about your luck, but the deal is off. I'm taking the ship back ... and no refunds."

The alien looked closer at the barrel of the weapon and then at his three unconscious companions and the one writhing in pain with an arm that was spasming out to his side, overcome by the electricity coursing through his limb.

"I accept your terms."

"I thought so. Have you taken anything from the spaceport, or is it all still here?"

"Nothing has left the spaceport. We intended to keep the vessel, but first, we had to remove the miscellaneous trash—eh, personal items—that were not of consequence."

"You just better hope nothing got broken. And now, you and your spastic friend over there will put everything back in the ship. Don't bother putting it away; just get it aboard. I want to leave this shithole of a planet as soon as possible."

"Yes, yes. Immediately, although Yaris will not be of much help."

"The others will wake up in a few minutes; they'll help. Now, get to work."

For effect, Adam pulled the MK away from the alien and let him watch as he dialed the intensity up to Level-2. Then he looked at the alien and grinned. "In case any of you piss me off."

From the look on the creature's face, Adam was sure *pissed* didn't translate properly, but the alien got the message. He gathered up his companion and together they began carrying boxes back into the *Arieel*.

Adam went to the flatbed truck and sat on the back. He removed a long stick of peanut butter taffy from his utility belt and began tugging at the tough candy, pulling away the breathing mask for each twisting bite. He loved the stuff, which was impossible to find anywhere in the galaxy except his homeworld. It cost a small fortune to have the candy shipped in from Earth, but it was worth every credit.

Eventually, the stunned aliens came to, and after a few seconds of heated explanation, they joined the other two in placing Adam's *'shit'* back in the *Arieel*. When they were done, Adam waved his weapon and sent them scurrying across the landing field. They wasted no time putting distance between themselves and Adam. Perhaps it was his departing words that made them hurry.

"If I ever see any of you again, I will kill you where you stand. Is that understood?"

They understood.

****

Once everything was back inside the ship, Adam climbed into the pilot seat and linked with ground control. To his surprise, the same controller as before came on the screen; a native called Hasson Kri, if Adam remembered correctly. The alien raised a bushy eyebrow when recognizing Adam.

"I need clearance to lift," Adam said.

A sly grin crossed the face of the native. "That will be six hundred energy credits."

"Six hundred! Why so much?"

"Let us call it an *inconvenience* fee. There have been reports of gunshots and a disturbance on the field. I assume that was you. Such acts cannot be tolerated on Ryndon."

Adam stared at the controller with unblinking eyes. It lasted almost a minute before the alien spoke again.

"Transmit the payment card now, or you cannot leave."

Adam continued to stare.

"Is there a problem with the link?"

Adam slowly shook his head. "No, there's no problem with the link. I just don't think I heard you right. Do you know who I am?"

The native tried to give a confident snort, but it came off as more nervous than confident. "I am a veteran of spaceport operations. Yes, I know you to be a Human, although I have not seen your kind on Ryndon for many years."

"You know I'm a Human, yet you still want to charge me six hundred credits as a departure fee?"

"Humans are no longer a force in the galaxy; you should know that."

"I do, but there's one sitting only a few miles from your workstation, *Hasson Kri*. That doesn't concern you, even after the reports of a *disturbance* on your field?"

The air traffic controller's confident façade was fading quickly under the intense glare of the Human.

"Perhaps—out of respect for the past achievements of the Human race—I can offer a discount ... fifty percent. Three hundred credits."

Adam continued to stare.

The alien swallowed hard. "Or even more, a one-time pass off the planet ... at no charge."

The corners of Adam's mouth curled up. "That's mighty generous of you. Send the departure vector and I'll be on my way."

Hasson worked his computer.

Once the coordinates were in the nav computer, Adam smiled, blatantly baring his teeth at the frazzled native. The creature shuddered on the screen, telling Adam that his species bought into the belief that baring one's teeth was a death challenge rather than a smile.

"It has been a pleasure doing business with you, Hasson. Even so, you should hope you never see me again. I get pissed off easily."

Hasson heard the translation of *pissed off* in his ear but was too scared to question the incongruity.

"Have a pleasant journey ... away from Ryndon."

Adam nodded and cut the link.

Chapter 5

Once again, Adam was to the point of frustration ... and boredom. He was away from Ryndon and headed to the planet Tel'oran on the outskirts of the Juddle Nebula and the headquarters of Starfire Security. The problem: It would take three weeks to get there. As a man of action, this sitting around and watching old videos or reading books he'd read a dozen times before was excruciating.

He went to his stateroom and took off his shirt and shoes. Adam looked at his image in the mirror, reacting—as everyone who knew him did—at his strange appearance. Before him was the toned and muscular body of a mid-twenties, blond-haired man looking to be in excellent physical condition. As an ex-Navy SEAL, that was to be expected. He'd always prided himself on his conditioning and worked hard to keep it that way.

The dichotomy came from the fact that Adam Cain was fifty-four years old.

At least his mind was.

What he was looking at was the *cloned* body of Adam Cain, a miracle of alien science that had brought him back to life, giving him a do-over and resetting the clock back over thirty years. However, while undergoing the cloning process, the procedure was interrupted, ending prematurely when his growing body was only in its early twenties. That was fortuitous enough, but when it was discovered that the cloning was still taking place—albeit at a much slower pace—that's when things got really weird.

With his body still growing, injuries healed magnitudes quicker, and he didn't feel pain as intensely. This combination of beneficial side effects allowed him to tolerate the beating by the Anarean police officers and for his injuries to heal faster. Adam was assured these *secret powers* would eventually end once his body reached the natural end-stage of the cloning. When that would be, no one knew. But it meant that Adam was not only a much younger version of himself but also an ungraded model. At least temporarily.

It wasn't supposed to be like this, but who was Adam to look a gift horse in the mouth?

Deciding that he was once again too young to retire and lead a more sedentary life—as most of his older friends had done—Adam decided to continue a life of adventure in the galaxy rather than return to Earth. The decision was often satisfying, at other times, disappointing. Adam loved the thrill of the hunt, particularly the bashing of alien heads. But these long, boring lulls between the action made Adam regret his decision.

Of course, there were other reasons why he didn't want to return to Earth, at least not now. But mainly, it was because Adam loved using his new body against much weaker alien baddies he encountered along the way.

At one time, he'd been ready to call it quits, conceding that thirty-plus years of traveling the galaxy and engaging in countless wild adventures were behind him. And then came the cloning. The fact that he had to die before being cloned *was* a consideration, but Adam didn't dwell on that. What he chose to dwell on instead was his new lease on life and the opportunity it gave him to chalk up more thrilling adventures as Adam Cain: *The Human*.

He laughed, thinking how others often saw him: as the quasi-superhuman hero of the Human race. Of course, he saw the legend from a different perspective, one filled with pain and suffering, alongside some incredible victories and a deep sense of satisfaction for all he'd accomplished.

Even so, Adam was grateful for his new body and the second chance it gave him. And he intended to make every second count ... when he wasn't bored out of his skull enduring three-week journeys through the nothingness of outer space.

Well, at least he could catch up on his sleep.

With the *Arieel* on autopilot, Adam lay on his bed, staring up at the ceiling until his eyelids began to flutter. Five minutes later, he was asleep. And oh, what dreams did Adam Cain dream....

41

Chapter 6

Names within the Milky Way Galaxy were often a confusing subject. Was the planet called Tel'or or Tel'oran? And was the nebula it was in called the Juddle or the Silvean? It depended on who you asked, a native or an *Outer*.

Why Tidus chose the planet for the headquarters of Starfire Security was anyone's guess, but it did have its advantages. It was more-or-less centrally located within the borders of the old Expansion and on the side of the galactic core with the Far Arm, where Earth was located. But the location wasn't that important. With Continuous Wormhole communications, anywhere in the galaxy was only a link away. And Adam was seldom on the planet anyway. As the only Human on the payroll, he was constantly in demand, which was both good and bad. Tidus wanted to take all assignments, while Adam preferred to pick and choose. He was only one man and couldn't fulfill every contract tendered. Tidus had ninety-eight other agents—and growing—but once the word was out that Starfire had a Human for hire, Adam was all anyone wanted.

Adam couldn't complain. Tidus treated him well—almost like a partner rather than an employee—and the pay was good. But it did run Adam ragged.

Tel'or—or Tel'oran (Adam preferred Tel'oran)—was an eight-level technological world which put it solidly in the *civilized* classification and with all the amenities one would expect. Adam had spent considerable time here throughout the years and knew the capital city of Dal Innis well, although nowadays, he called the *Arieel* his home. He had a permanent landing pad at the executive spaceport about ten miles from Starfire headquarters, complete with a private transport for when he was in town.

After landing—and making sure the ship was locked—Adam took his car to the business district of Dal Innis to meet with Tidus in his office/home.

The seven-foot-tall, green-skinned Juirean with the starkly angular face and four-foot-long white ponytail greeted Adam with warmth and sincerity. They'd known each other for a long time and had shared many an adventure together. These days, Tidus was too old for field work. Besides, he was making a killing as the owner of Starfire Security, thanks mainly to The Human's reputation. He didn't need to get his hands dirty to make a fortune.

"Hey, look at this," Tidus began as Adam plopped down in a thickly padded chair on the other side of Tidus's desk. The alien went to a refrigerator and pulled out a can with a blue and red logo Adam instantly recognized.

"No shit!' he exclaimed. "*Pepsi!* Where the hell did you get that?"

"Not only Pepsi, but Diet Pepsi, your favorite." Tidus handed him the frosty can. Adam opened it immediately and then choked a little as he gulped the highly carbonated soft drank.

"Seven thousand credits to have ten cases shipped in," Tidus explained. "I love the stuff, too, and I figured if you're willing to spend the bucks on peanut butter taffy, I could splurge on some Pepsi."

Adam raised the can to Tidus who had just popped a top on a can himself.

"To the good life, my friend," Adam toasted.

"To the good life! And in your case, to a good *second* life."

"Jealous?"

"Who wouldn't be? But that's water under the bridge." Tidus walked around the huge stone desk and sat in a chair that could be easily confused with a throne. He was making good credits in the security business and spared no expense on his creature comforts. He held up the can again. "To another mission accomplished. The

Zanoreans are happy, we've been paid, and you got your ship back. What could be better?"

"How about something outside the Quadrant where I'm not so recognized. Besides, I need to catch my breath. Twenty apprehensions in six months. That's a lot."

"It is, and your damn pay and bonus money is piling up."

"I've been too busy to notice."

"That's what I get for having a Human for hire. Everybody wants a piece of *your* action."

"Have you thought about bringing on another Human?"

Tidus finished off his Diet Pepsi and went for another. Adam declined a second, knowing Tidus only had a limited supply.

"Hell, I would, if I could find one. I thought you guys were scarce three years ago when we started this gig. But now, it's like finding a needle in a haystack."

Adam smiled and shook his head. "There you go again, Tidus. If I'm not mistaken, you've never been to Earth, and yet you talk just like a Human."

Tidus snickered. "Hey, watch the insults, buddy! But seriously, I like to study my enemy, at least back when Humans were the enemy of the Juireans. Besides, I have a knack for languages, and your English is one hell of a fascinating language. And I read a lot, mostly Human writers. I love that guy, T.R. Harris. You know he has a grammar-checking dog if you believe that. You ever read anything by him?"

Adam shook his head. "Can't say I have. Now, back on topic, do you have anything coming up that could be classified as simple?"

Tidus grinned, baring his teeth at Adam. Juireans didn't subscribe to the baring teeth/death challenge thing. They didn't have to. For four thousand years, his race ruled the galaxy. If they wanted someone dead, it wasn't a challenge. It was just done.

He checked his computer. "I've been looking while waiting for you to get back, and I have something for you specifically A simple escort job. Have you heard of the Binary Conference that's taking place soon?"

Adam shook his head.

"Well, it's a big trade bruhaha where about two dozen planets here in Sector 12 are getting together to reestablish more secure trade routes between their worlds. As you know, after the invasion, things have been a mess, with the space lanes mainly controlled by pirates and the cartels. Product is moving, but at too high a cost for these guys. This is the first step in getting things back to normal."

He sipped his Pepsi before continuing.

"Needless to say, the bad guys are all up in arms about this and have vowed to stop the conference at all costs. The delegates are hiring teams of security personnel to escort them to and from the venue."

"What about during the conference?"

Tidus nodded. "Binary is being held on a space station near Ladhi. A large security force has already been hired to protect the station. All that's needed is to get the delegates there and back safely."

"How big of a team are you sending?"

Tidus held up a single finger. "Only one ... you."

"Why?"

"It seems we were underbid on the larger teams, and the one client left is not in a position to afford more. Our client is a Lep'sorian. His planet is up and coming but nowhere as wealthy as the others. Not all the participants are rolling in dough. When they learned I had a Human for hire, they jumped at the chance. You're a bargain when compared to what the others are charging for five- and ten-agent teams."

"But only one person guarding this guy when the others have larger teams?"

"Don't worry. The Lep'sorians are way down the ladder when it comes to potential targets. Hell, they would probably try getting there on their own if it wouldn't make them look even poorer than they are. And advertising the fact that they have a Human guarding the delegate, well, that adds a little pizazz to their mission."

"How much?"

"Ninety thousand ECs, round trip. The trip from Lep'sor to the conference will take two days, and then the conference lasts for five. Nine days total for ninety Kay, not bad."

"And my cut?"

"The standard forty ... plus an extra five for babysitting duties."

"What does that mean?"

"You'll see. Let's just say the delegate is not quite mature yet. His race is kind of strange. You'll see when you go to Lep'sor to catch the flight on their official state cruiser."

"There better not be diapers involved," Adam said seriously. "Especially alien diapers. If so, then I want a full twenty percent bonus. When do I leave?"

"Three days. Gives you time to relax, do a little shopping, and polish that super weapon of yours. I didn't ask, but did you get a chance to use it on Anarea?"

"Once. Blasted a hole clean through some alien asshole."

Tidus frowned and recoiled. "Hey, be careful, Adam. I *resemble* that remark."

"Which one, the alien or the asshole?"

"Actually ... both."

They laughed and toasted again with their precious cans of Diet Pepsi.

Chapter 7

The planet Lep'sor was a three-day journey from Tel'oran, which gave Adam time to do some research on the planet and its inhabitants. After Tidus's cryptic remark about the maturity of his charge, Adam was curious what he meant. He searched the files of the galactic Library, the internet for the Milky Way created and maintained by the Formilians. The Library contains the largest database of information in the galaxy and was free to all those with a linking code.

Adam was mildly shocked when he read about the Lep'sorian race.

Most races within the civilized part of the galaxy were classified as *Primes*, the designation created by the Juireans thousands of years ago that basically referred to beings like themselves. Humans were solidly Prime, although from the Human perspective, these creatures would be called *Humanoid*. The Lep'sorians were borderline Prime, and some of the most exotic aliens Adam had ever seen, although their form and lifecycle had their parallels on Earth.

They were basically tadpoles and frogs, although much more advanced along the evolutionary scale. The tadpoles—which were called Neos—were about six feet tall, walked on two legs, had a pair of articulated arms with three-fingers-and-a-thumb hands. They had wide, flat faces with two solid black eye beads about the size of racquet balls resting atop their heads and broad lips that could express a variety of emotions. They had both gills and lungs, and moist skin that both excreted and then absorbed a thin, viscous liquid. Rounding out the tadpole comparison was a long, fin-like tail.

But this was only when the species was in the Neo stage. At about age twenty-two, they would transition into a much hardier and muscular form of creature resembling a nightmare version of a giant frog called a Borr. This new version was about seven feet tall with powerful hind limbs, a pair of shorter front legs and then a separate set of arms out in front. The face and skin was knobbier and dryer than the Neos and gone were the gills and tail. The Borrs were impressive looking things, and not something Adam would want to tangle with.

But then came the strangest revelation. The Borrs didn't run the society. The Neos did.

Around six years of age, the Neos were capable of advanced reasoning and intelligence and began assuming their duties as the leaders of the race. They were the intellectuals, the politicians and the entrepreneurs. At the same time, the Borrs were the laborers, almost mindless grunts who did the farming, worked in the factories and provided security for the planet.

For about six months before the transition, the Borr would grow within the skin of the Neo until it contained two complete bodies with two brains. Some of the knowledge and intelligence of the Neo would be passed to the Borr, but not all of it. It was an upside-down arrangement, where the older, more robust form of the species was dumber and less creative. The older a Lep'sorian became, the less it contributed to society.

Adam had never seen anything like the Lep'sorians before. And Adam's assignment was to protect a senior Neo named Kimm Jors. Each of the twenty-seven worlds participating in the conference was allowed only one delegate. Even their staffs were limited to three assistants. The event was more of a meet and greet, and then a signing ceremony for agreements that had already been worked out ahead of time, and not by all twenty-seven member planets, but by the big five Elites, the wealthiest and most powerful in the Sector, including the delegate from the planet Tel'oran. Adam was surprised to learn that Tidus had lost out on providing security for the Tel'oran delegation, seeing that his company was headquartered on the planet. But there were older, native organizations that got the contract.

Adam was glad he wasn't on that side of the business, where politics played as big a role as did price and ability. Tidus reveled in the contest of wills. Good for him. Adam was done with running point on operations. He just wanted to be given an assignment and then left to his own devices to carry it out. And when it was done, it was done. No lingering entanglements after a job. Just get it done, get paid, and move on. It fit his new perspective on life.

****

Adam landed on Lep'sor and was greeted at the spaceport by a single Neo who would take him to meet with Kimm Jors. As soon as Adam stepped from the *Arieel*, he was slammed with a wall of oppressive heat and humidity. The planet was not so much a water world as it was a *marsh* world. On the ride into town—in a transport without air conditioning—all Adam could see were lakes, ponds and slow-moving rivers crossed by a dozen bridges. Towering palms and other large-leafed trees grew on the edge of the water features and even rose from their depth. Animal life squawked and/or flew throughout the jungle and it was here that Adam saw his first Borr.

They were diving in the water, often in large pods, and with Neos standing atop huge barges. The Borrs were bringing up baskets of black mud and depositing them on the barge. The driver—a Neo—noticed Adam's fascination with the dredging operation.

"Our chief exports are cadmium and lithium," he explained, sounding articulate and intelligent—for a giant tadpole. "Most is mined from below the surface. We also produce and export a variety of organic products created from the mosses and seaweeds that are abundant on Lep'sor."

"It seems to be labor intensive," Adam said, wanting more information about the Borrs.

"We find it more cost effective to use manual labor in the dive operations. Although the Borrs have lost the ability to breathe underwater, they can still stay submerged for up to thirty standard minutes. They also have incredible endurance and can work for many hours non-stop. And besides, they enjoy being in the water, as do all Lep'sorians."

Adam wanted to tell the driver how much he could relate. After all, Adam was former Navy SEAL, a job he'd aspired to since he was nine years old. But he held back. It would require too much explanation to bring everything into context.

The marshy jungle landscape soon gave way to a massive clearing that was free of most of the larger trees and built on solid ground. There were a myriad of buildings, some not more than mud domes, others high-rise affairs climbing twenty-five stories or more but also covered in what could only be described as dried mud. This was confirmed on a dozen of the structures as crews worked adding fresh layers to the sides that dried quickly in the intense heat.

Adam was taken to one of the larger buildings where the driver parked the vehicle and then personally escorted Adam inside. There were mostly Neos in the building with only the occasional Borr moving about. When inside, the Borrs tended to walk on their four legs instead of the two massive hind legs. They could do that, too, and without difficulty. It was just that inside the building it was easier to move about presenting a lower profile and not scraping the ceiling with their knobby heads.

The pair entered an elevator and were whisked to one of the top floors where another Neo was waiting, this one much bulkier than the driver and wearing a wide, friendly grin. The Lep'sorian offered his hand in the form of a traditional handshake.

"I am Kimm Jors," he said amicably. "I am quite honored to meet a Human in person. Honored, indeed."

Adam took the moist, warm hand and shook it, bowing slightly as he did. "I'm Adam Cain, and it is I who am honored. I understand you are an elite member of Lep'sorian society and the delegate to the Binary Conference."

"It is a birthright, not gained from ability, I assure you."

The driver laughed. "Do not let his humble ways fool you. Vis Jors is a senior member of the government, an accomplished merchant and a distinguished intellectual, what others call a scientist. He is well-respected on Lep'sor, and hence his appointment as a delegate to the conference."

Kimm placed a hand on the shoulder of the assistant. "I keep Kriscroz around just so he can sing my praises. It would sound egotistical should I say these things about myself."

Adam chuckled, instantly taking a liking to both Kimm and the Lep'sorians.

"I hope you had a pleasant journey," Kimm spoke. His black orbs moved up and down Adam's body, with transparent eyelids occasionally closing and opening as they coated the eyes with fluid. "I understand our climate can be difficult for most outsiders. We will be moving to the ship momentarily where it will be possible to localize the temperature and humidity. You will not have to endure this much longer."

"I'm fine, *Vis* Jors," Adam said, using the formal address for the delegate. "This humidity is good for my skin."

Kimm laughed. "As it is for ours, as well. Come, let me take you to meet the others. I am allowed only three companions, and Kriscroz is one. He is my most valued adviser and is soon destined to assume my role in the affairs of Lep'sor."

"Soon?" Adam asked as he walked alongside the much larger native. "Are you ... I don't know, retiring?"

Kimm's big head nodded. "That is one way to look at it. In truth, I am at the end of my Neo stage and will soon be transitioning. It is two weeks away, so this conference will be my last official act. Perhaps you have researched our society, Vis Cain? From my experience with others from the Expansion, ours is a *unique* makeup."

"I know you change form. Beyond that, I don't know much."

"It is more than just form. We are essentially replaced by the next stage in our development. In two weeks, Rion will emerge and I will be gone."

"Rion?"

"The entity that is currently growing within me. Surely, you have noticed the size difference between me and Kriscroz."

Adam had so many questions but didn't know how to ask them without sounding insensitive. "I guess, what I'm curious about is what becomes of you when Rion appears?"

"A part of my consciousness will live on in Rion, but not much. In your context, I will die and Rion will continue."

"And you're okay with that?"

Kimm laughed. "It is how Lep'sorians have evolved over a million years. It is our way, and we accept it. I have spent a long and valued awareness serving my species. I welcome the end."

"And Rion will take over—" Adam stopped abruptly, remembering what the Library said about the Borrs, about them being essentially dumb beasts of burden.

"No, he will not. That will be the job of Kriscroz. It is why our different stages have different names, different personalities. As I said, it is how it has always been. Until our people joined the Expansion over eight hundred years ago, we knew nothing of how life evolved on other worlds. Now that most of us are aware, we can see why we are considered different. As I said before, we consider ourselves *unique*, more than different. Our metamorphous from Neo to Borr has served us well. It allows us to contribute to our society while in a young and fresh form, and then continue to contribute in a simpler, yet just as important way."

As they entered another room, Adam shrugged. "Of course, I'm fine with that. To each their own, as Humans say. It works for you."

"Yes, it does."

There were two other Neos in the room, each looking younger and more slim than Kimm. They wore expressions of genuine thrill at meeting Adam. One even giggled.

The corners of Kimm's wide mouth curled up. "Forgive Rado, she has heard so much about Humans throughout the years that to actually meet one is a thrill. It is for all of us."

Adam waved his hand. "There's no need for you to feel that way. We're just like you. We evolved on a world that made us who we are. Nothing special about that."

"I beg to differ," Kimm said. "We have been members of the Expansion for hundreds of years and never achieved the rapid success Humans have in your relatively short time on the galactic scene. That is why I am honored to have you as my escort and my protector. I could not have wished for a more capable being other than yourself for such a task."

"Just remember, Vis Jors—"

"Call me Kimm."

"Okay, Kimm. And you can call me Adam. But I want you to remember that I work for *you*, not the other way around."

"I realize that. But please forgive us a little hero worship. It is not every day that one meets a Human."

Kimm went on to introduce his third assistant, a native named Galcik. After that, Kimm received last minute instructions from the Leadership Council and then led Adam and the three natives out the building to a waiting passenger van. Adam's duffle bag of equipment was already loaded aboard and they set out for a different spaceport, this one for executives and government officials.

Thirty minutes later, they were in space and closing in on one of the largest starships Adam had ever seen. He stood at the forward viewport of the shuttlecraft gawking at the magnificent vessel.

"It is the pride of our fleet," Kimm said from beside Adam.

"It's friggin' huge!" Adam exclaimed.

Kimm chuckled. "I appreciate your attempt to modify your speech for my benefit, Adam, but it is not necessary. Lep'sorians swear more than most species. Perhaps you will get to hear some during our time together."

Adam was still entranced by the starship. It was oblong in shape with at least thirty focusing ring pods along the forward section. There were hundreds of portholes and other viewing windows along the shimmering silver hull and a variety of landing bays set in the aft section. It was every bit as large as a Juirean Class-7, the largest warship ever built, with the exception of a Klin Black Ship. Those Behemoths were six miles long.

But even as impressed as he was with the vessel, it seemed out of step with the humble Lep'sorians. Kimm noticed Adam's frown.

"We call it the MOB-4, and please consider, Adam, that the Lep'sorians are not of the mainstream of galactic society or accomplishments. We have been trying to break into the upper echelons and were making progress when the Klin invasion occurred. That has set us back. Hopefully, this conference will open more opportunities for us to resume our upward mobility. That is a long way of explaining why we have built the largest non-military vessel in the galaxy—that we know of. It is because we must present a façade to others, a way of proving we belong here. Call it insecurity, but it is real. We have seen how others react to us, and when we show up in the largest starship of any of the delegates, it will be noticed." He grinned, showing off an incredible row of tiny white teeth—at least a hundred of them lining both plates of his enormous mouth. "It is the same with you, Adam Cain. We may not have been honest with your employer; we could have afforded more security personnel. But that would have only diluted the uniqueness of having the only Human in any security detail. And putting my faith and security into the hands of a single being also shows our courage and trust in our decisions."

It took a moment for Adam to absorb what Kimm just said. It was great that he trusted the Human's skills, but Adam was being used also as a publicity stunt, telling all the other delegates that the Lep'sorians didn't need *more* security personnel, only the *best*. And that was The Human. It put a lot of pressure on Adam not to screw up.

"Well, I don't know what to say about that. I'm just one person. In reality, I can only do so much."

"I realize that. I am not asking you to do more than you would do for any client. Besides, I don't anticipate any hostilities toward my mission. Lep'sorians were an afterthought to the conference organizers. Even so, we want to make an impression. Please don't fault us for using your fame—the fame of your race—for a little selfish gain."

Damn, Kimm was a smooth one, Adam thought. He wanted to be mad, even a little insulted, about being used. But he couldn't. He understood what the Lep'sorians were trying to do. Adam had been around enough pompous and arrogant leaders and races that he could relate to the lowly Lep'sorians. Fine, let them use him for a publicity stunt. Adam would play along; in fact, he'd overdo it some, just to help Kimm out.

But first things first.

"I'll do my part," Adam promised much to the delight of the delegate. "But I still have a real job to do. The cartels are serious about stopping the conference, and if not stopping it, then disrupting it in some way."

Kimm nodded. "Yes. Recently, they have been earning credits by offering escort services for trade vessels within their territories. This requires merchants, such as me, to pass the extra cost onto our customers. By establishing set and protected trade routes, routes which can be guarded by the new police force being formed, we can save credits, lower prices and provide a better standard of living for billions of creatures. The cartels and pirates are not anxious to see their hold over the Sector lessened. They will fight to keep what they have."

"That means every delegate is in danger." Adam raised his hand to stop Kimm's protest. "Even if you don't think you're in any real danger. But as I said, I have a job to do. The journey to the station is two days—"

"It will take three in the MOB-4." Kimm looked embarrassed … if a tadpole could look embarrassed. "Our vessel may be large, but it is also slow and grossly underpowered. It was not built for speed, only for show."

Adam grinned. "Okay, then, three days, which will make you even more of a target. I need a station set up on the bridge with all advanced warning beacons slaved to my controls. I also asked for some monitoring drones."

"They are aboard," Kimm confirmed.

"Good. I want them set out a couple of light-years from the ship as an early-warning system. I'm hoping you have weapons systems aboard, both offensive and defensive."

"We have the standard energy shields and plasma cannon. Honestly, we have not taken the ship out on too many voyages. It is quite expensive to operate."

"I can imagine. But we'll take it easy and keep an eye out. But if something comes up, I will need operational control of the ship."

"I will inform the captain. Much of this has already been discussed. We are in conformity of thought."

"Excellent," Adam said.

He'd been watching the massive starship grow larger by the minute. Now they were there and the true size of the behemoth was apparent. The MOB-4 was built to impress, and that it did. Adam just hoped it could fight if the chips were down.

But then again, who would want to harm the lowly Lep'sorians?

Chapter 8

Good to his word, Kimm had the captain designate an area on the bridge for Adam. He had screens with navigation, weapons and a threat board. They launched the four drones Adam had asked for and sent them out to two light-years forward and aft, port and starboard. The ship's sensors reached out that far, but the drones gave them an extra light-year of coverage. It wasn't much, not with an enemy ship coming in on a deep gravity-well, but it would provide a few extra seconds to launch countermeasures.

The fact that there could be an imminent attack set Adam and the crew on full alert, something they could handle for a seventy-two-hour stint. Even so, Adam popped a few stay-awakes, determined to stand watch the entire time. He could sleep during the five days of the conference. On the trip back, he would relax the threat level some, thinking that any attack by the cartels after the conference would just be sour grapes rather than any strategic purpose. They would probably reserve such attacks for the responsible parties, the Big Five, who put the conference together.

Kimm wasn't kidding about the ship being slow. It had six huge gravity generators and thirty focusing rings. Even still, it could barely make one hundred light. Adam also tested the reactive controls and found those lacking as well. The MOB-4 turned like an overweight manatee negating any possibility of out maneuvering an attacking warship.

As Adam sat in the darkened bridge, manned by a skeleton crew during what was the Lep'sorian night, he hoped everyone was right, that the tadpole/frog aliens weren't worth the effort to attack. Honestly, he didn't know what he could do if they were. He'd checked the lifeboats; they were adequate for the number of crew aboard. He also mapped his quickest route to his assigned boat ... just in case. Not that he was planning for the worst. But he was.

The first day and night went by without incident. But by mid-day of the second, Adam was receiving reports of attacks on other delegates. Some of the attendees took longer to get to the venue, others less time. But by now, nearly all the representatives were on their way, making for a target rich environment for the raiders.

Two delegate ships were destroyed, while another three were able to fight off the attackers. Some of the wealthier attendees had not only hired muscle but also escort fighter ships. They came out of the engagements without a scratch. Adam recorded the attacks and studied the tactics used by the cartels and the pirates. It seemed the two evil parties had linked up, since stopping the conference was in both their interests. That complicated the matter while allowing for engagements over a wider area. By the end of the second day, four more attacks had taken place and another two delegates were down.

The organizer of the Binary Conference got on a joint link and extolled the attendees not to give in to the terrorist activities. He was a Velosion and one of the Elites. He was followed by words of encouragement from the other four, including the floppy-eared representative from Tel'oran. Even so, a couple of the delegates called it quits and turned back for their homeworlds. But most continued. Out of the original twenty-seven, four were dead, and two retreated, leaving twenty-one to continue to Ladhi.

****

It was early morning on the third day, with groggy Lep'sorians trying to make it through another mid-watch. Adam was right there with them. He'd taken as many pills as he dared and now two days without sleep was catching up to him. Although his body was that of a young stud in his mid-twenties, the lack of action was also taking its toll. He could go for days if he was in the heat of battle. But the boredom was weighing on him as well as the hours without sleep.

And then one of the outer drones began to ping. The ominous tone snapped Adam wide awake. He snapped his fingers to get the attention of the Leps—as he'd come to call the Lep'sorians. They responded as expected—for aliens—sluggish and confused.

Adam called up the sensor.

It was from the aft drone, which wasn't surprising. Anyone monitoring the lumbering starship could measure its speed. Hell, most shuttlecraft could go faster, if they had the range.

Adam primed the flash cannon and set the aft screens at full. The cartel ship would see the screens pop on and know they'd been spotted. It might be enough to deter an attack.

But then the starboard drone began to ping.

Adam scrambled, adjusting the shields while charging another bank of cannon. The cartel/pirate ships weren't coming in with their usual hair-on-fire bravado. Instead, they were approaching leisurely, almost nonchalantly. Did they know the capacity of the MOB-4? That could be a problem, although Adam did have an ace up his sleeve.

Kimm was on the bridge a few moments later, along with a full complement of bridge crew and the captain. They seemed to know what they were doing, at least when it came to flying the MOB-4. But it was a safe bet none of them had taken the massive space slug into combat. Strange, pollywog-like faces kept looking at Adam for guidance.

"Captain, can you hail the incoming ships?"

"Pardon, the translation was inadequate."

"Can you link with them? I want to speak with their captains."

A few seconds later, two screens lit up and a black-skinned alien and one that looked yellow appeared.

"This is the MOB-4 out from Lep'sor. Can you state your intentions?"

The black-skinned alien took the lead. "I believe you are aware of our intentions. However, we will not attack your vessel should you come about and return to Lep'sor. We will give you two minutes to comply. Otherwise, we will initiate an attack."

Adam looked to Kimm. He looked different, his wide mouth stern and his black eyes even more intense than normal. Even his voice was deeper when he spoke. "We will not turn back. We will not be intimidated by thud-fuckers."

Adam was surprised the translation bug found a suitable equivalent in English to the Lep'sorian curse word. He was also taken aback by Kimm's intensity. This was another side of the Lep'sorian he hadn't seen. He looked angry.

"Very well," Adam said. "In that case, I am taking control of the ship. Steer 120, up 10." This sent the MOB-4 to port and up slightly from the prior level course. At the same time, Adam took manual control of the drones.

After precisely two minutes, the dual cartel ships powered up and sped in faster, not waiting for a verbal confirmation of the Lep'sorian's intentions. They paired up, one in the lead, the other his wingman.

Adam was in a quandary. He would have to dump out of the gravity-well to fire his weapons. The enemy knew this, and they could force the issue by overloading the well on their end by firing plasma bolts forward of the MOB-4. The bolts would be caught in the influence of the well and be sucked into the singularity. The series of black holes at this point were a finely balanced mix of dissolving and emerging gravity points. The cannon fire could disrupt that, causing the ship to lose well-integrity, at least momentarily. The problem was the uncertainty of when and where this would happen. Adam preferred it to be on his terms, not theirs.

He dissolved the well and the ship fell from light speed. The raiders were on them in an instant, having also dropped out of their wells. Cannon fire erupted and a moment later impacted the energy shields. There was little damage; the first few salvos in a battle were mostly harmless, feeler shots just to get distance and lead time. The shields worked not by deflecting the plasma bolts but by absorbing them. But they could only absorb so much. After that, they had to power down and vent the energy. That could be terminal in the heat of a major battle.

Adam lit off a series of cannon fire of his own. The same thing happened on the enemy ships; they didn't give a damn, not for another two or three hits and then on a single shield. Excess energy could be transferred between shields, keeping the most vulnerable screens going a little longer.

"Shield integrity holding," the captain called over to Adam. He was a professional. There was worry on his face, but his voice was strong and confident.

Adam kept lighting off cannon fire at the two ships. They were aft of the MOB-4 and staying in formation. They didn't seem to be in a hurry to cause damage to the massive starship. Instead, they were toying with it.

In the meantime, Adam was quickly working the drones. They had all fallen back behind both the MOB-4 and the cartel ships. Adam timed their movements to the hits from the MOB-4's cannon on the enemy shields, knowing that for a split second, all sensors were blinded by the bolts. He was bringing them ever closer.

The cartel warships kept steadily poking at the huge bear of a starship, loading up a shield before changing the target area and going for another screen. Eventually, it would kill the huge beast, but it could take fifty cannon bolts or more. It was slow-motion murder.

Adam had had enough. The drones were about a quarter-light behind the cartel ships when Adam engaged the gravity drives on the four drones. Instantly, their signatures showed up on the screens of the cartel ships, but they were too close to get away. The wells formed forward of the drones, catching the enemy ships at the other side of the spherical gravity-well, if not sucking them in, then keeping them from engaging their own singularities.

And then the drones struck. Normally, this would have caused a fair amount of damage but not critical, like a fifty-five-gallon drum shot from a cannon and impacting the side of a building. What made these impacts more serious was that Adam had each of the drones filled with a thermite-type explosive of alien design. The drones were flying mines and they easily obliterated the cartel ships, creating a glowing fireball that, because of the distance and the speed of light, would take forty-eight seconds to reach the MOB-4. By then, the bridge crew already knew the outcome of the battle, thanks to their subspace sensors.

Leps came up to Adam and patted him on the back—the universal sign of congratulations. He'd saved them; there was no doubt about that. The problem: Adam only had four explosive-packed drones, and they were all used up. If the cartel launched a second attack on the MOB-4, they wouldn't have a chance. But they were now seventeen-hours from Ladhi. The chances of the cartel attempting a second attack were slim to none. Adam relaxed and looked around the bridge for Kimm. He hadn't come over to congratulate Adam, and he was nowhere on the bridge. It seemed odd.

Then Adam laughed to himself, thinking how ridiculous his thoughts were. First, he had no idea how to read Lep'sorian emotions. And secondly, Kimm was going through some major personal changes, what with another creature growing inside his body and his impending death, timed almost down to the minute. That had to screw with a person mentally, if not chemically. Adam still liked the alien. He would cut him some slack for not responding exactly as Adam expected him to.

Besides, for the time being, Adam was the hero of the MOB-4. And knowing the Leps—as little as he did—he knew they would play this up with the other delegates. Where four attendees died in cartel attacks, the Lep'sorian's sole Human saved their VIP. It was just another feather in Adam's cap, and worth another ten thousand ECs on his next contract. He would be sure to tell Tidus so the extra fee would be reflected in his bonus.

Chapter 9

The MOB-4 made it to the Ladhi system with no further incident and joined up with the chaotic cluster of ships forming up around the conference venue. It was an old Juirean Spot Station, a space station the aliens once used as a temporary base of operations as they moved about the Expansion, and in areas where they didn't have land bases. Such stations hadn't been in use for fifty years or more, but this one looked to be brand new. Adam learned that it had been sold to the Ladhi a decade ago to serve as a posh resort around a unique double-ringed planet in their system.

From where Adam sat on the bridge of the MOB-4, he could see the unbelievably beautiful planet in all its glory, being one of the most awe-inspiring sights he'd ever seen in space. The rings were very Saturn-like, but with two of them spinning in tandem and separated by about twenty degrees of arc above the swirling kaleidoscope of clouds making up the planet. It was as if Jupiter had double rings. Adam thought it was Saturn on steroids, with a little LSD thrown in for good measure.

The glorious sight lit up the space station and its gaggle of transport liners, reflecting every color of the rainbow off their shiny hulls. Adam could see why not only the Ladhi, but other tourists from across the galaxy, would flock to the station. Because of the unique nature of their most famous attraction, the Ladhi spared no expense rehabbing the old station and turning it into a showcase. It was not only a luxury five-star hotel in space, but an all-inclusive resort as well. It was the perfect venue for the Binary Conference.

The station itself was a slowly spinning wheel in space, looking to Adam like all the old drawings of 1960's space stations created by science fiction visionaries. It was called Rizen Station after the spectacular glowing world it orbited. There were hundreds of windows set in three rows circling the station, and the spinning of the station afforded each room a breathtaking view of the planet every thirty-eight minutes.

The delegate transports were sequestered to the far side of the station from the planet and were packed in much too close for Adam's liking. There were easily fifty vessels—including the extra fighter escorts some of the delegates brought with them. The ships were of a variety of makes, but mostly luxury liners designed to carry their VIP passengers in style. Even so, none of them compared to the MOB-4. First of all, the other ships were not particularly large, just opulent. They were dwarfed by the mass of the Lep'sorian cruiser. Adam held his breath as the captain maneuvered the behemoth close to the others—too close. But the captain knew his ship and stopped short of any collisions, but close enough for the other delegations to marvel at the scale.

Adam grinned. Although he couldn't see the reaction of the other attendees, he knew the Lep'sorian's evil plan was working. How could it not?

****

Adam had his duffle bag of equipment with him, ready to board the shuttlecraft for the Station, when Kimm came up to him. This was a different Kimm than the one he'd last seen on the bridge during the cartel attack. This was the congenial, easy-go-lucky Neo Adam had first met. He wondered if Kimm was going through a form of alien metamorphosis as he came closer to transitioning. It could explain his mood swings.

It didn't matter; this was the nice Kimm, and that was good enough for Adam.

"So, we made it here without incident," the Lep'sorian said joyfully.

Adam frowned but let the comment slide. Perhaps he meant without any deaths—except for the cartel and pirate crews. In that case, he was right.

"I have checked the itinerary; there is a dinner tonight for the security and advisory personnel in the B-14 serving hall," Kimm began. "At the same time, there is a delegates-only feeding in A-3 followed by an informal mixing event. I know not what these location designations mean, but I have a map. But first, we are to be shown to our quarters."

"I was told about the dinner," Adam confirmed. "If you don't mind, I'd like to leave my equipment in your room until I find where I'll be staying."

"Of course. And what treasures have you brought?"

"They are hardly treasures ... unless one is fighting for his life. Just a few bolt launchers and ballistic weapons, along with ammo, battery packs, sensors and other detectors. Everything a growing soldier-of-fortune may need."

Adam watched Kimm as the translator worked through his Human-speak. In the end, Kimm perked up.

"Ah, soldier-of-fortune! That is an apt description of your profession. Do you find the work satisfying?"

Adam shrugged. "It's the thing I was trained to do, so I guess it must be okay. I've been doing it for a very long time."

It was hard for a Neo to frown, but Kimm managed. "I do not know of the aging process for Humans, but I get the impression you are more of a Neo rather than a Borr."

"Looks can be deceiving, Kimm," Adam said cryptically. "Perhaps on the way back to Lep'sor I'll tell you my story. But right now, there's not enough time. Besides, you wouldn't believe me if I told you, not without a lot of intoxicants and convincing."

Their conversation was cut short by a call to board the shuttle. Only five people left the MOB-4; Adam, Kimm and his three assistants. The flight took ten minutes, most of which was spent maneuvering through the traffic and entering the huge landing bays of the Station.

****

Adam was mildly shocked by the incredible press of flesh in the bay. He should've known, what with approximately two hundred security personnel dwarfing the number of delegates and their staff. Add to this the station personnel and the private security team that was hired to protect the Station, and there were easily five hundred people moving about the huge chamber looking for directions.

Ladhi natives, wearing reflective red jackets, stood along the periphery of the room holding up signs in the native language of the delegates. Kimm spotted his and Adam followed. Along the way, he saw a phalanx of stern and serious armed guards wearing uniforms and standing off in the wings, not milling around with the others. This would be the on-site security contingent—Unidor Security. He also didn't know how many there were; it was a big station. But having an extra two hundred hired guns wandering the halls could be a pretty good deterrent against any direct cartel action toward the conference.

For his part, Adam didn't like being in crowds, especially alien crowds.

He was mostly shorter than everyone else making him standout. This was the result of Humans having evolved on a heavy gravity world, but unlike others with such pedigree, Adam's race had learned to fully function in the oppressive gravity, even excelling in it. Most heavy-worlders were low-slung, sloth-like creatures that could barely tolerate their own planet let alone function beyond it. This is what made Humans so unique. They made the most of the extra muscle and quickness their heavy gravity upbringing gave them while being on Juirean-Standard worlds. It was a mild form of superman-ism, without the flying and being immune to bullets.

The other reason Adam didn't like crowds was because someone would invariably recognize him as a Human. That was the case here, especially among the security personnel. This was a competitive business, reeking of alien machismo, and anyone who had been in the field for more than a few weeks knew of *The Human*. And now, here he was among them. They were curious, if not disappointed, to see him in person.

Adam shook his head and grinned slightly, seeing the variety of alien expressions on the cascade of strange faces. He could almost read their minds.

"So, that's a Human? ...Not very big, is he? ...There must be some trick to his success. ...He does not look that tough."

One or two steely glares his way was bad enough, but in the landing bay, there were dozens, if not hundreds. Eventually, some macho jerkoff would try to test his skills against Adam and then there would be a fight. It always worked out like that.

And that was why Adam was anxious to get to his room, where he could hibernate for the next five days. Mingling with his fellow soldiers-of-fortune would only lead to trouble.

The Ladhi attendant led Kimm's small party down a long, slowly curving central concourse, then up a ramp escalator and along more corridors and intersecting hallways before entering an elevator. Adam tried to keep track of where they were going, but after a few extra turns and down passageways that looked the same, he gave up. They walked on plush, carpeted floors, and along the walls were strange works of *art*. Some were interesting, if not pretty. Such was alien art to a Human rube. Very little of what aliens considered beautiful did Adam agree.

Eventually, the party was moving along the outer edge of the station in an area separated by doorways spaced a hundred feet apart. When the attendant stopped and unlocked a door, Kimm and the others were presented with a room featuring a fifty-foot-long picture window that faced out at the incredible double-ringed planet. The timing was fortuitous, as the Station continued to spin. The four Leps and one Human stood mesmerized. Although they'd seen the planet from the MOB-4, it seemed the station's window might be more of a magnifying glass than a simple window. The rings looked proportionally closer and the colors more vibrant.

Adam was also greeted with a blast of heat and humidity.

"This is the main suite," the Ladhi explained with pride. "The Delegate has the Blue wing, and the others, the Yellow. We have studied the living environments of all our guests and have customized the rooms accordingly. If there are any other special accommodations you need, please signal the service staff. The pre-meal social gathering will begin in an hour. The Station will announce the event at that time. Mealtime will commence an hour later. Native attire is appropriate. Please enjoy your stay aboard Rizen Station. Gratuity is not required."

When the Ladhi left, Kriscroz, Rado and Galcik rushed to the Yellow wing to check out their accommodations. Adam could hear them gushing from the great room.

Adam followed Kimm into the Blue wing, instinctively checking the room for ingress and egress, defensive positions and concealment points. Kimm wasn't concerned with any of that. Instead, he marveled at the size and luxury of the apartment, which is what it was. The space had to be fifteen hundred square feet with a sunken bed jetted with nozzles for water to enter. This might be how Neos slept, submerged in water since they had gills to breathe. The Ladhi were sparing no expense pampering the conference guests. Adam was sure they wouldn't go through this much trouble for the security details.

He tried to imagine what the kitchen in a place this big would be like, and with such a varied clientele. He'd hate to be the one in charge of hundreds of different native dishes. Thank god for computerized processors and food paste.

"I'll just drop my bag in the living room," Adam said, excusing himself while Kimm looked in every nook and cranny in the room, fascinated by what he found. Although he was rich by Lep'sorian standards, this must be more than he was accustomed to. As a race concerned with superficiality, this room was almost a sexual experience for the Leps. Adam felt it best to leave them to their simple pleasures.

Besides, he had his own room to find. He left the suite for the hike back to the landing bay.

Rizen Station had been emptied of all guests other than conference personnel. That meant even the staff was reduced, since the normal occupancy of the resort was over five thousand. Now, Adam couldn't see more than five to six hundred being aboard, including wait staff. As he walked along the wide corridors, he didn't see a lot of people except for the occasional Delegate party being led to their room. Some of the aliens would sneer at him, not because he was a Human, but because he wasn't dressed in some gawdy finery such as were they. Few of the attendees were as humble and down-to-earth as the Lep'sorians; in fact, most were real snobs.

It took Adam almost half an hour to find the landing bay again, and when he did, he discovered that most—if-not all—of the security personnel were still there. None had been taken to their rooms, confirming his belief that that would happen after dinner. Even so, there was a general atmosphere of unease and a lot of alien grumbling.

Adam looked around for someone he could ask about what was going on. There was definitely something out of the ordinary happening.

He caught the eye of an exceptionally short alien bodyguard wearing a tight-fitting leather bodice lined with weapon holsters that identified her as a female—a very tough female. She was standing off to the side of others wearing the same colors if not the same design of garment. There were four of them, all of different species, including a Rigorian. That was the signature look of freelancer units. They came from every society and congregated in a couple of dozen major companies and twice that many minor firms that had sprung up since the Klin invasion. Teams seldom consisted of the same species; in fact it was a rarity.

The alien female grinned at Adam, careful not to display her teeth. This could be from caution. Even Adam wouldn't be quick to show his pearly whites in a crowd like this.

He moved over to the female. Although he noticed how short she was compared to the cohorts, next to her she was every bit as tall as Adam at six feet. She also had a fine female figure, bronze skin and blondish hair. Her face was cute, if not pretty, in an alien kind of way with larger-than-Human dark eyes, a smallish nose and generous lips. Seldom did Adam find aliens attractive, but this one was the exception.

Adam opened his mouth to introduce himself but the alien spoke first.

"You are *The Human*, are you not?" The voice was pitch-appropriate for a female and spoken with an air of confidence. Although there were many races with accomplished female fighters, the security industry was still dominated by what would be classified as males.

Adam nodded. "I am."

"Idera Jemor; we are from San'nor Protection."

"Starfire Security."

"I have never heard of you."

That was fine., Adam thought. He had never heard of San'nor Protection, either.

Adam looked around the room. "I stepped out for a moment. What did I miss?"

Idera nodded. "Then you did not hear that all security personnel are to return to their ships after the dinner."

"Why?"

"It is by order of the Station security force. They are to be the only ones aboard responsible for the protection of the delegations."

"Again, I ask why? We have a whole army of bodyguards here."

"I concur. But we were told there would be too many overlaying command points and decision makers. There is to be only one, those from Unidor Security."

Of course. Unidor was a pretentious organization calling themselves the new unifying police force in the galaxy. In the wake of the Klin invasion, there was no organized police or military authority spanning star systems. The Juirean Expansion was gone, as well as the Human Orion-Cygnus Union. These entities—and others—maintained a level of universal law and order respected by most civilized worlds in the galaxy. But with them gone, others were stepping in trying to fill the void. Some approached security as Tidus and Adam did, one client at a time, and taking on work mainly from private individuals and smaller governments.

Unidor was billing themselves as the new galactic police force and the Binary Conference was their first true test. As part of the agreement between the twenty-seven worlds involved, Unidor was to become the accepted law enforcement agency between the systems, with authority to carry out operations on any of the worlds. It made sense. The galaxy was too diverse and spread out to leave law enforcement up to each individual system. There was too much intermingling of people and commerce. Eventually, it would either be a new galactic empire along the lines of the Expansion, or it would be a police force like Unidor. That still didn't excuse their uppity attitude.

This placed Independents like Adam at odds with the upstart *FBI* agents of the galaxy, Unidor Security. Adam had tangled with their agents a couple of times before, mainly over jurisdiction, for which they often claimed dominion over territory they had no right to claim. They also considered themselves above people like Adam, who took assignments as bodyguards, bounty hunters, mercenaries and even hired muscle if the job paid enough. He and Tidus would work for any side in a dispute, whoever was paying the bills.

And now it was Unidor who was responsible for internal security aboard the Station. And there would be no way they'd let a bunch of amateurs with guns wander the corridors of their Station.

"I hope they know what they're doing," Adam said to Idera. "This is a big station and the cartels are determined. How many are there aboard?"

"I do not know, but the number that has been mentioned is twenty-five."

"Only twenty-five?"

Idera nodded. "Hardly enough in my opinion."

She looked over at her companions. They had noticed her talking with Adam and were coming over.

"Who is your new friend, Idera?" asked a seven-foot-tall lizard Adam recognized as a Rigorian. He'd had a lot of interaction with the beasts throughout the years, mostly bad. In fact, the first alien he ever killed was a Rigorian. Adam smirked at the thought. *You always remember your first.*

"This is The Human; I have forgotten your name," she said to Adam. He hadn't told her.

"The Human is fine. Just call me Human." There was a possibility the Rigorian would recognize his name. As mentioned, he'd had a lot of interaction with the species in the past.

"Perhaps the two of you have bonded, both being small and insignificant."

"Caution, Kalc," said another of the team.

"Yes, I know of the Humans, more than most," the Rigorian snapped. His foot-long snout with double rows of inch-long teeth jutted out toward Adam, the corners of the mouth curling up. "If the Klin did anything right, it was to cancel out the arrogant attitude and ambitions of the Humans. But now this one shows up, and if the stories are true, he single-handedly saved the life of his client, and in that obscene hunk of a starship the Lep'sorians think will show their worth.

It is a shallow and transparent effort, which includes the hiring of *The Human*. You are but a tool and a tiny one at that."

A bell chimed, and a voice came over the intercom. Adam heard the words in English as his translation bug deciphered the Ladhi speaker. Everyone in the room was hearing the words in their native language.

The pre-meal mixer was about to begin. Ladhi guides would direct the mercenary army to the meeting room, where the meal would follow soon after. But then afterward, they would all be required to vacate the Station, by order of Unidor Security.

Adam wanted to skip the mixer and even the meal. He could get something to eat back on the MOB-4. But none of the Station shuttles were leaving, not until after the meal. The Lep'sorian shuttle had returned to the mothership earlier, believing that Kimm and his party would be staying for the full five days. His team would. But not Adam. There were Station shuttles being prepped to ferry the mercs back to their respective ships. Adam wasn't looking forward to that, either, being crammed in an open bay in the back of a shuttle with a couple of dozen other bodyguards. And he knew the MOB-4 would be the last ship the ferry would service. After all, it only had one passenger to deliver.

Reluctantly, Adam followed the crowd out of the landing bay and down the first-level corridor. He learned that the main hallway was the C Concourse. Above it was the B, and then the A was reserved for VIPs. This was where the Delegates would be meeting and having their meal. It was also off the A Concourse where Delegate's Row was located.

Adam grimaced, remembering that his duffle bag was in Kimm's suite. He had planned on moving it to his room once he found out where it was. Now, he'd have to get it after the meal and before the last shuttle left the Station. Maybe by then the ferry traffic would be thinned out, leaving him more or less alone for the trip back to the MOB-4.

Adam noticed that Idera was staying close to him and not to her team. She had a sour look on her face and Adam could guess why.

"They don't respect you much, do they?" he said to her as they made their way to the meeting room. "I get it. I've known quite a few Rigorians and they can be real assholes."

Idera snorted. "I am glad our languages are compatible for the translation of *asshole*. You are correct. He truly is. To him, only size matters. I am every bit the warrior he is, but because I am smaller, he does not consider me a part of the team. And being senior, he has either ignored me or given me the shit assignments."

Adam grinned—not smiled. "I like you, Idera; we speak the same language, sort of."

"Us runts must stick together."

They shared a laugh, during which it was okay to display their teeth. The emotion was better understood than simply baring ones teeth at another.

Once they were in the room, they were left alone. Although everyone knew what Adam was, the other mercs refused to treat him special, preferring ridicule over respect. He and Idera made idle talk, sharing stories of their recent assignments. Idera was a Cos'minean, a race Adam had never heard of. Of course, he didn't tell her that, since she knew a lot about the Human race.

"I was once an officer in my planet's defensive force. We made a good effort against the Klin, but in the end, there were just too many of them. A Human force came to our defense, but they, too were repelled. The Klin were using their jump ships at the time. There was little we could do against them."

Adam nodded knowingly, but he didn't tell her how much he knew. That would have freaked her out if she would even believe him. He preferred to remain as anonymous as possible. Not invisible; that was impossible. But no one needed to know his true background. Being simply known as *The Human* was good enough.

"I know not with you," Idera began, "but does something seem strange about this conference, and especially the security setup? It seems we are being watched as if we were the enemy. We are both experienced operatives. Does this seem right to you?"

Adam smirked. In police circles back on Earth it was known as JDFR—*Just Doesn't Feel Right*—that itch you get on the back of your neck when things seem out of kilter. And here he was, twenty thousand light-years from Earth and with an alien ex-cop who was expressing the same uncertainty. It had to be a sixth sense people like Idera—and Adam—shared.

"Yeah, I feel it, too. Twenty-five agents are far too few to guard the Station. And not taking advantage of the firepower you have available also doesn't make sense. I can understand the possibility of a splintered chain of command, but that's something that can be worked out. They're not even trying."

"And the Unidor beings; they cause tingles within me. And not the good kind." Idera's actual smile was delightful. Of course, she only showed it to Adam.

"There's one of them over there," Adam said, referring to the Unidor sentries. In fact, there were several of them in the room. They seemed to be standing guard more than being a part of the fraternity. *Arrogant assholes*, Adam thought.

He and Idera went over to the closest one. Adam had watched as a couple of the others had come up to him and made quick reports. He seemed to be the leader or at least high-placed lieutenant. The officer was an imposing figure, although he was only about six-and-a-half-feet-tall. His arms were like metal girders and his face seemed to be made out of stone. He wore the customary black and dark green uniform of the Unidor Corps, as they tried to make themselves look more like an army rather than a rag-tag group of mercenaries.

"Hi, there," Adam said cordially. "We were wondering why Unidor doesn't take advantage of the skills you have available in this room to help augment your force, There doesn't seem to be enough of you for the job." Adam tried not to come off sounding critical, but with an alien, one never knew.

The creature stared at Adam with unblinking black eyes. There was intelligence behind them, and he used them to size up Adam, along with his female companion.

"You are The Human," he finally said. And that was all, nothing else.

"Yeah, that's right," Adam acknowledged after a few seconds of awkward silence. "And who are you?"

"I am Endic Vor, the Captain of the Unisor Defense Force, and I assure you, my unit is adequate for the task at hand."

Adam could tell he'd insulted the alien. "I'm sure it is, and with a couple of hundred armed agents sitting only a few hundred miles off the station, I'm sure no one would dare attack the conference. It's just that we're all being paid to protect our clients, and most of us take our responsibilities seriously. It would be nice if you'd let us do our jobs. And it would save you from having to do it for us."

Now, the officer grinned. "Your *jobs*? You are nothing but hired amateurs who are more a danger to your clients than any of their would-be enemies."

Adam recoiled. "That's kinda harsh, isn't it? You're no different. You're here because you've been hired to be here, just like us."

"We are nothing like you. We are here because we are to be the unifying law enforcement agency in Sector 12, and soon the entire galaxy. Someone has to provide law and order, and mercenaries like you are only delaying the unification."

"Eventually, governments will unite, and the empires will reform," Idera offered. "There was order in the Expansion before the invasion, even though most worlds were independent and free to form their own police and military."

"And how did that independence serve us during the Klin invasion? We were overwhelmed by a more organized enemy."

"It was a little more involved than that," Adam said

"How so?"

Adam didn't want to elaborate. He had information very few in the galaxy knew. "It doesn't matter. What matters now is that the Klin invasion failed and we've been left with a mess. My friends and I serve a vital need, making sure the bad guys are brought to justice no matter where they go."

Endic Vor batted his eyes several times as the translation worked through Adam's Human slang. When he finally had the gist of the comment, he laughed.

"A simplistic version of reality. But that is exactly why Unidor will succeed." He looked at Idera. "Until your favored governments unite, there will be a need for someone to bring order to the disorderly. That is what we are doing. And people like you—and the Human—are operating beyond the law. You are no better than the criminals you hunt. And I assure you, if any of my force would encounter your kind in the field, we will treat you as the common criminals that you are. Is there anything else you wish to discuss before you are fed and then depart my Station?"

"It's not your Station," Adam said pointedly. "It belongs to the Ladhi."

Endic shook his head. "For the next five days, it belongs to me."

Idera took Adam's arm and pulled him away.

"He is beyond salvaging. He has been seduced by Unidor propaganda."

Adam walked away, but he kept looking back, his eyes and those of the alien meeting in a long-distance contest of wills. Dammit, Endic

Vor was one of the reasons Adam hated aliens so much. Well, most aliens. Idera seemed to be okay.

****

Idera and Adam were now joined at the hip. With nothing to do for the next five days, she didn't feel obligated to sit with her team when the meal was announced. She seemed more comfortable with Adam, and he with her. She was the only thing that made the meal tolerable.

The wait staff came around and noted the seat numbers before offering blood sampling boxes for the guests. With a quick prick of the finger, the computer knew what food and drink would be compatible for the species. It was a standard practice throughout the galaxy, and one Adam insisted on. He didn't want to die from alien food poisoning. So far, the system worked. Adam was still alive. Well, he was ... again.

Surprisingly, Adam wasn't offered a menu of compatible meals, so he shouldn't have been surprised when the waiter brought back something that resembled a hamburger. Apparently, the computer researched Human food and found a hamburger was the most popular. Adam would have preferred a steak, or even chicken. But a hamburger it was. Or what the computer estimated a hamburger should taste like. Mushy cardboard with catsup was a better comparison. Even so, by now, Adam was starving. He did his best to swallow the faux burger, washing it down with a passable intoxicant resembling beer. The beer was the best part of the meal.

But then it came time for everyone to pack up and leave. Idera's eyes still darted around the room, and a frown was perpetually painted on her forehead.

"I still feel something is not right," she whispered to Adam. "It is giving me concern."

Adam felt the same, although he didn't know how much of it was sympathy worry because of Idera. Still, the Unidor officer had grated on him. That could also have something to do with his feeling of unease.

"I'll catch a later shuttle," he told Idera as he walked her to the landing bay. "I left some things in my client's room. I'm going back to get them."

She was barely listening, the worry now consuming her. They said their goodbyes, with Adam thanking her for saving him from an evening of unbearable boredom ... and possibly a fist fight or two. She said the same to him. There were no hugs or kisses. After all, they were aliens. That would have been disgusting.

Chapter 10

The room where the Delegates met and ate was a much fancier and better-appointed chamber than where the security teams met, with an expansive ceiling decorated with original paintings and chandeliers made of glowing points of lights Kimm knew to be sustain energy bolts. He tried not to show his wonder at the splendor displayed and how nonchalantly some of the delegates absorbed the atmosphere. This is what he envisioned for his race—someday. But for the time being, they would remain on the sidelines, looking in at an existence they could only dream about.

Kriscroz, Rado and Galcik were just as impressed, and Kimm had to tell them to maintain their demeanor. He didn't want them to standout any more than they already did. He wanted to act as if they deserved to be here, in this room, at this conference and within this strata of galactic society. Even if they didn't.

The mixer was awkward. Kimm did chat with a few of the other delegates, ones he knew were only a step or two above the status of the Lep'sorians. All the others ignored them, at least to a point. Condescending glances were cast their way and Kimm heard mumbles about the gawdy starship brought to the conference for show, nothing else. *It must have cost a whole year of planetary economic output to build,* he heard someone say, just before the laughing began. The sad truth, they weren't far off. Perhaps bringing the MOB-4 wasn't such a good idea.

And then the meal came, which was from the staff of the Rizen Station and not from the conference sponsors. It was served with pomp and ceremony and with no distinction of class. Kimm and his people were served at the same time as all the others, which did not sit well with a few of the delegates at nearby tables. And where two to three sets of delegates would share large tables, as they ate, discussed and laughed, the Lep'sorians sat alone at a smaller table.

Kimm knew his place. His people had been copied on the various working papers during the pre-conference negotiations, but it was simply for information. They had no input. In fact, very few of them did. That was left to the Tel'orans, the Avions, the Galin-Noc, the Moreans and the Vandash teams on their respective planets. It was implied that the Elites—the Big Five—would go it alone if the others in the Sector did not abide. The attitude was, 'Be glad you will be included in the final agreement. Other than that, you will have no input.'

And that was Kimm's attitude. It would be a start. Lep'sor would be part of a twenty-seven-world alliance, out of the three hundred nineteen Prime worlds that had been part of Sector 12 when the region was with the Expansion. The planet would be forever a part of the upper echelon, even as others fought to join.

The Neo did not concern themselves with immediate gain, which may seem strange considering their short lifespans. But because it was short, they tended to think ahead to the next generation and the next. There wasn't time to make radical changes before they would transition. Everything was done incrementally and for long-term effect.

The Borrs were somewhat different. Although of limited intelligence, they did seek out more material gains. That was why they worked so hard in the mines, harvest fields and factories. They strived for more, living in communal groups and sharing most of what they made. This could have something to do with the fact that they were responsible for the constant birthing of Neos. It could be paternal instinct that drove them, needing to provide a safe environment in which to lay their eggs and nurture them to birth.

At that point, Neos took over. It was the way it had always been.

****

After the dinner, the representatives for the Big Five got up to speak. They laid out the progression for the conference, detailing how each

Delegate would be assigned to a working group that would go over a portion of the agreement, asking questions and being provided with answers until they fully understood their responsibilities and what they could expect in return. There were to be no amendments to the agreement, only understanding. These groups would rotate between other parts of the agreement until all were versed in its meaning and consequence. On the morning of the fifth day, there would be a symbolic vote for ratification, after which the closing mixer would take place.

Kimm had already read the full agreement, as had all the Delegates. To him, it seemed like an incredible waste of time going over it again in such detail. But it was a process that had to be followed. The organizers didn't want any of the planets coming back later saying they didn't realize a certain provision was in the agreement. Kimm accepted the rationalization. He was an accommodating creature.

At one point, a representative of Unidor Security was asked to speak. He was a high executive and not a part of the local security force. Kimm took interest in what he had to say, after all, the primary purpose for the conference was to join forces against the cartels and pirates to provide more secure trade routes. That was in the agreement, but almost as a side note. Most of the document dealt with tariffs, taxes, fees and other minutiae that would take place between trading partners. Most worlds already had such regulations. The conference would standardize a lot of it.

But the police aspect interested Kimm the most.

The concept was simple, if not the implementation.

There would be one police force for the Sector, a quasi-military outfit called Unidor Security. They would have stations on each planet and patrols in space along the established trade routes. They would be responsible for protecting commercial and private vessels along these routes, as well as having the authority for law enforcement on all of the signatory planets. Each world could still maintain a local police force and military, but by signing the agreement, each world would accept Unidor as the higher authority. This was so no criminal could escape justice by simply running to another world in the Sector, as it was now. Under this new agreement, the criminal element would find the Sector an inhospitable place to conduct business and be forced to move elsewhere. At least that was the intent.

Kimm looked around the room. Over the past few minutes, more Unidor soldiers had moved in, standing along the perimeter looking impressive in their black and green uniforms. Kimm saw this as a demonstration of the new look of Law and Order in the Sector for generations to come.

In a way, it was comforting; in another, a little scary. That meant there would be Unidor soldiers on Lep'sor and probably recruited from locals so they could better tolerate the climate.

The only concern Kimm had was who would ultimately be in command of this new police force. It was said the coalition of planets would have control, but this was a private company they were hiring. At some point, many worlds would decide to forgo their own police and military forces, finding the need redundant and the costs unnecessary. At that point, only Unidor would have the guns. And they were loyal to no single government, only to the credits that flowed into their accounts.

Kimm decided to leave that worry to the next generations of Neos. His time was at an end, and he needed to trust his fellow Lep'sorians that they would know what to do in the future.

Chapter 11

Adam was lost, hopelessly lost.

Although there were color codes everywhere, he was confused what they meant. There were translation stations every few hundred feet along the corridors, but unless he knew what to ask for, they weren't much help.

And there was no one around. All the security details were being shuttled off the station while the dignitaries were at their fancy shindig somewhere in the A Section. And, of course, the A, B and C Concourses weren't color-coded, just the different features of the Station, such as the pools, the restaurants and the gaming venues.

Adam had worked his way up to the A Concourse; he knew that was where Delegate Row was located. But it wasn't along the main corridor. Even so, he knew which way the Station was spinning letting him know the direction to the outer hull and the magnificent suites reserved for the VIPs. He knew Kimm's room number, but that's when another issue came to mind.

He didn't have a key. If Kimm was still at the dinner, he'd have to wait for him to return. Adam shrugged. If he missed the last shuttle, he'd just have to crash on Kimm's couch and try to get back to the MOB-4 tomorrow. He was pretty tired, still recovering from the long watch he'd pulled on the way to the conference. A couch would be just fine. More than fine, in fact, considering how plush everything was in the suite.

****

Adam gave out a sigh of relief when he saw a Unidor security guard come out of an elevator. He would know the way to Suite odd-symbol, odd-symbol three hash marks and a circle. Adam had no idea what all that meant; everything was written in Ladhi. But the security agent should know.

Adam raised his hand while calling out to the agent.

"Hey, am I glad to see you! I need some help finding my room."

The guard had turned away from Adam when he exited the elevator; he must have been startled because he turned with his Xan-fi rifle pointed squarely at Adam's midsection.

"What are you doing here?"

"I'm trying to find my room. I left some stuff in there."

The guard looked Adam up and down.

"It is not your room. You are not a Delegate or of a delegate staff."

"Yeah, you're right. I'm with a security detail, for the Lep'sorians. I just need to get my bag before I go back to my ship."

"You are not supposed to be here."

"I realize that," Adam said. "And as soon as I get my bag, I'll return to the landing bay, no delays."

Adam heard the bell on the elevator chime and the door began to open. Adam stepped back to let whoever was in the car exit. He grinned cordially, expecting to greet a returning Delegate to the Row.

Instead, he saw three white uniformed wait staff lying on the floor, still smoking holes in their bodies from recent flash bolts. They were dead, with the leg of one of then tripping the open-door sensor.

Adam turned in shock to the agent—the same agent who only seconds before left the elevator.

The beast was huge—as they all were—and had his weapon aimed at Adam. A Xan-fi at this distance—and assuming even a Level-2 bolt—would be deadly, even for a Human. Rifles carried more punch than did handguns. And they didn't use targeting computers, they were made for long distance shooting, or for more deadly attacks.

Adam spun away just as the weapon discharged, sending a blue-white plasma bolt zipping past his midsection. At the speed of the bolts and the blinding effect they had on eyesight, it looked more like a beam than a single point of light, making it easier to see how damn close Adam came to getting his gut shot off.

But now he was in defensive mode, stepping to the guard's right and closing the distance in a fraction of a second in Human speed. The alien reacted, swinging the Xan-fi and striking Adam across the side of the head. The creature was strong and quick, quicker than expected. The agent brought the rifle stock up and slammed it into Adam's chin and then shoved the weapon into his chest pushing him into a credenza set against the opposite wall of the corridor.

Adam's focus blurred for a moment and he went into a clench, much as boxers did when they needed to calm things down and regain their senses. Then Adam's hand found a decorative glass vase on the table. He crashed it into the alien's head sending glass shards cascading over both the fighters. The hulking creature didn't even bat an eye. He continued to press the rifle into Adam while working it back and forth, jamming the stock into Adam's belly and the barrel into his head.

Using the credenza as a backstop, Adam pushed off, making the huge beast stumble backwards, surprised by the strength of his much smaller opponent. Then Adam swung his right arm down on the hands of the terrorist, dislodging the weapon from his grip. It flew across the hall landing ten feet away.

Now the combatants squared off against each other. The alien wore a confident grin backed up by this extra foot of arm's length. Adam went into his best Mike Tyson imitation, clenching his fists and holding them close to his head while bobbing and weaving. He was quicker than the alien, but not by much. What was superior, however, was his reaction time. The beast telegraphed his punches by first cocking his arm and then letting off the slow, meandering roundhouse punches, which Adam was easily able to avoid. And then Adam went on the offensive. He first struck the side the alien's torso with a strong right hand. It made an impression. Then he followed up a split second later with Tyson's favorite punch, the uppercut. Being shorter than most of his opponents, Iron Mike loved to punch up, out of the blind spot of the other fighter, catching them under the chin. That's just what Adam did. The alien wasn't expecting it and flung his beachball size head back with a snap. That's when Adam followed with a left cross to the temple, or what would be a temple on a Human.

The beast was shaken and confused. He stumbled back, holding his long arms out in front as he shook his head, trying to clear the cobwebs. But Adam was just getting started. He ducked and barreled into the chest of the alien, pummeling his midsection with a rapid succession of eight blows, alternating between rights and lefts. The creature buckled over, which put his thick chin directly above Adam's head. A quick lifting of his head made solid contact with flesh and alien bone, sending the beast toppling backward to the floor.

Adam stood over the mighty beast, panting and still slightly dazed. The creature was still breathing but lay unconscious. Adam recovered the Xan-fi and then relieved the terrorist of his MK-17 bolt launcher, along with an extra battery pack for each weapon.

Further rifling of his pockets revealed an official-looking card with the Rizen Station logo on it and a back of electronic circuitry. It was a room key but a little fancier than the one Adam saw with Kimm. Curious, Adam went to the closest door to one of the luxurious suites and swept the card. To his delight, the door unlocked. Either it was an incredible twist of fate that this just happened to be the terrorist's room, or Adam was holding a master key to all the suites and maybe more. Seeing that the alien was part of Unidor's security team, it made sense that he would have a master key.

Adam thought for a few seconds what to do. It was obvious this beast was a Cartel plant, sent here to disrupt the conference. But how many were there and how exactly were they going to carry out their plan?

With an unlocked door to an empty and inviting luxury suite, Adam returned to the sleeping alien and dragged him into the room.

He propped him up on a couch and then looked around for something to tie him up with. There was a fancy set of drapes at the massive picture window with thick corded draws. Adam went over and pulled on one of them, ripping the entire drape off the wall in the process. Exasperated. He placed a shoe on the fabric and pulled on the cord again. This time it broke away.

He had about twelve feet of rope, which may or may not be enough. He started with the creature's thick wrists, making sure to double and triple band them. Then he moved to the ankles. They were about a foot in diameter, and out of caution, Adam pulled the second drape from the wall and gathered another twelve feet of rope, doubling up on everything he'd just done.

After that, Adam spent more time going through the beast's utility vest and other pockets and compartments, looking for ID or communication devices. He had an earpiece as well as a chest monitor. Adam took both of them. They looked to be standard Unidor issue equipment, so he wasn't sure if the Cartel would be communicating with him through these devices. They may not be communicating at all, having given him instructions and setting him loose. The only thing Adam was sure about was that he wasn't alone. There were too many Delegates, and the Station was huge. If the Cartels wanted to make a point, they'd do it with more than one assassin.

The agent was still unconscious, and Adam was getting impatient. He went into the spacious and well-appointed kitchen and got a glass of water. He tossed the liquid in the alien's face. Nothing. He was really out.

Adam got a second glass, and when this one also failed to revive the creature, Adam leaned over to check his pulse. And that's when the damn beast tried to bite him. Only Adam's lightning-quick reflexes saved him from losing a finger.

Adam jumped back as the beast began thrashing around on the couch, tugging at the bindings and even chewing on the ones on his wrist. Adam firmed his jaw and stepped up to him, holding a clenched fist a few feet from the alien.

"Do you want to go another round?" The confused looked told Adam he didn't understand. But when Adam feigned a punch, the alien recoiled. "Yeah, *that* you understand."

Adam pulled a chair over and sat across from the couch, close, but not too close.

"How many of you are there aboard?" The alien snapped his mouth shut. "C'mon, I know you're not here alone. What are you supposed to do for the Cartels? I know it's more than killing a few service workers."

The red eyes of the alien—yes, red; that was unusual, even for aliens—looked genuinely confused, although Adam had learned long ago not to jump to conclusions regarding alien body language.

He sighed, figuring he'd have to do the interrogation the old fashion way, by brute force. That was okay. It had been a while since Adam was on this side of an interrogation.

"Six, report."

The communication box Adam had removed from the terrorist squawked. Adam reacted a split second later, diving to turn off the open circuit.

"L4, JJ105!" the tied-up alien cried out.

Adam silenced the offending device and then glared at the satisfied-looking alien on the couch.

"They will be here in seconds," the gravelly voice announced.

"Who, Unidor?" Adam asked. "I'm sure they'll be shocked as hell to find out one of their own is working for the Cartels."

The guard smiled, baring his teeth in an undisguised death challenge. "Then you may remain. Our fight is not over, and my companions will make short work of you."

The confident grin on Adam's face evaporated. Did he transmit a code to the alien's Cartel partners or Unidor? He had no way of knowing. But seeing how relaxed and confident the agent was told Adam all he needed to know.

"I'd love to sit and chat, but I have another appointment on the other side of town," Adam said. That really confused the alien. However, the Level-2 bolt he placed into the agent's chest with the MK-17 left no ambiguity. There would be one less alien assassin roaming the hallways of the Station.

Adam was out the front door two seconds later and sprinting down the corridor.

He skidded to a halt at an unmarked, nondescript door set in the wall. It had a card reader next to it. Adam slid the skeleton key through the slot, and the door opened.

As suspected, it was a cold, unpainted metal hallway that led to a myriad of other cold, unpainted metal hallways; the lifeblood of any large hotel, shopping mall or entertainment venue, the hidden corridors where the staff could move about without being seen by the paying customers. Adam hurried down the passageway, first turning right at an intersection and then left at another, varying his course. It was designed to confuse anyone following him. In reality, all it did was get him lost. He checked for security cameras along the way and saw none. He also didn't see another soul, which was fortunate. In his current elevated state of agitation, he might have shot first and asked questions second if anyone suddenly appeared.

He was still on A Concourse but moving inward. The Station was a large spinning wheel with each ring spanning about half a mile in diameter. There was the open area in the middle before reaching the other side of the ring about two miles away. A half mile of livable ring allowed for innumerable side passageways, workrooms, storage areas and power stations, and within a couple of minutes Adam felt like a rat in a maze. Occasionally, he came to exits that opened to the public areas of the Station, which included pools, gaming venues and dozens of alien restaurants.

It was eerily odd that no one was in the corridors, either behind the scenes or otherwise, and at one point, Adam stopped to take inventory.

He had a Xan-fi flash rifle with two power packs and an MK with the same. He had a communication device that had gone ominously quiet, telling Adam that the frequency had been changed, assuming he might be listening. And he had a master key, not only to the suites on Delegate's Row but all—or most—of the internal doors as well. That was good. It also told him that if he ever found Kimm's suite, he'd have access. He really needed his duffle bag, especially now.

But his main quandary was uncertainty. He had no idea who out of the Unidor security team had been bought off by the Cartels. He'd be taking a risk approaching any of them without having the upper hand.

But there was one Unidor officer he was pretty sure wouldn't be on the take, and that was Captain Endic Vor, a company man/alien if Adam ever saw one. Adam kicked himself for not learning the location of Unidor's headquarters aboard the Station.

His other option would be to get to the landing bay and any last stragglers from the security teams. There was strength in numbers, even if the numbers hated him. They would hate to lose their clients even more.

And that's when one of the ubiquitous TV monitors on the walls, both in the public and private areas, came to life. It showed an overall view of a large meeting room, populated with flamboyantly dressed Delegates and their staff. A yellow-skinned alien in a Unidor uniform was speaking, appearing ebullient and energetic as he gave his speech. Behind him were Captain Endic Vor and two other Unidor officers. Adam stopped to listen. The monitor had come alive for a reason.

Chapter 12

"I am deeply honored that the Binary Conference and the attending Delegates have chosen Unidor as your official security agency. As the executive vice-president of operations, I can tell you my staff and I have worked tirelessly toward this very moment. We believe in the promise of unity and security that will come from this agreement, and I vow that the trust you have bestowed upon my company and me will be returned a thousand-fold. You are taking a major step in restoring the galaxy to its past glory. There has to be a starting point; the Binary Conference will forever be known as that point."

He turned back and waved a hand at Captain Vor and the other two officers.

"On behalf of our on-site representation, I want to thank you again for allowing Unidor Security to share in this glorious undertaking."

Captain Vor stood, as did the other two. Endic bowed slightly and waved his hand at the applauding crowd. Adam had to assume this was a live feed of the meeting taking place somewhere on A Level, possibly right down the hall from Adam. He had no idea.

The camera scanned the crowd, and there, toward the back, was Kimm and his three staffers, sitting at a smaller table by themselves. They were cheering, along with the others in the room.

Then the camera panned back to the podium, just in time to see the two other Unidor officers behind Captain Vor pull their company-issued MK-24s and shoot Vor and the executive in the back of the head. They quickly followed with the assassinations of the Station Manager and two of his assistants.

At that range, it was a repeat of what happened when Adam placed a bolt in the brain of an Anarean. A second after the shot, their heads exploded. It sprayed the podium and stage in a sickening mass of red and grey goo.

Screams and panicked squeals erupted in the room as nearly a hundred creatures of all shapes, sizes and colors shot to their feet and began looking for an exit. But they were stopped by the ring of Unidor soldiers who had their Xan-fis out and pointed at the ceiling. In unison, they let off a series of shots designed to get the attention of the panicking mob. Over the sound of flash bolts and the screams of the attendees, Adam heard a voice pleading for calm.

It was one of the Unidor officers who had shot the others. He was a tall, angular creature with grey skin and a goatee on his prominent chin. Adam had seen the species before. He was a Valasprin.

"Please, everyone, silence!" he called out, waving his hands in the air while still brandishing the MK. The sight of the gun did nothing to soothe already frazzled nerves. But eventually, the officer was able to get the room back to a semblance of calm.

"Please, take your seats again. If you look around, you will see that the room is secured by my soldiers. No one is leaving without my permission. Now, let me introduce myself. I am Sandon Amick, and before you jump to conclusions, none of my companions nor I work for the Cartels or the pirate organizations." He grinned and nodded his head. "Although I must admit, our objectives are more or less entwined. But unlike the Gradis and Nimblis Cartels, our purpose is not only to disrupt the conference ... but also to become fabulously wealthy as a consequence." Soldiers began moving among the tables with intent, telling Adam they knew where they were going. "To that end," Amick continued, "I will ask that Polandin Davinor representing the planet Avion please come join me at the podium."

****

Kimm knew after the first name was announced who would be called next, although not in which order.

The guards stopped at Polandin's table and waited for him to rise. One of his staffers, an impressive beast that looked more like a bodyguard than an administrative assistant, jumped to his feet and lunged at one of the Unidor soldiers. He was shot dead a second later, not even waiting for the targeting computer to lock on. Those at the nearby tables screamed and dived for the floor.

"Remain calm; I will go," Polandin said to the two remaining staffers and the others around the table.

"Next, could Salus Newin from Tel'or join us?"

The terrorist creature Amick continued, calling Rorus Lim from Gal'in-Noc, Danonoz Hal'onkin from Banndock Mor and Van Izz from Vandash.

They were the Big Five—the Elites—the leaders of the conference and of Sector 12 and the wealthiest of all in the room.

"And lastly, please join us, Kimm Jors from the planet Lep'sor."

At first, the name didn't register until Kimm realized he was talking about *him*. He was shocked beyond words, even actions, unable to move from his seat. There were gasps around the room as the haughty attendees began asking *why Kimm, why a Lep'sorian*? They were nobodies. It was as if the others *wanted* to be taken instead just to prove their importance.

Once the shock wore off, Kriscroz and Rado stood to protest. Rado was shot in the back before Kris quickly regained his seat.

Kimm nearly fainted at the sight of his trusted assistant lying smoking on the floor. She had been with him for most of his tenure as a lead Neo. He continued to stare at her, even craning his neck backward as strong alien hands guided him to the podium.

"Very good; the rest of you can relax. My associates and I are in complete control of this Station. All landing bays, receiving ports and lifeboats have been locked down. No one will be arriving or leaving until the game that is about to commence has been played out. The security personnel on the surrounding starships are to make no moves to gain entry to the Station, and no warships are to be brought in from Ladhi."

Amick walked along the row of dignitaries, still wearing his confident, almost amused grin.

"Now, let me explain what is to happen. Those standing before you will have the honor of being ransomed off to their respective governments for a sum of five billion energy credits each."

There were more gasps within the crowd, but not much. Those still left in the audience were just glad it wasn't them. Kimm was still questioning why he was there. Lep'sor did not have a sum total of five billion credits in all the coffers and financial institutions on the planet. It would be impossible for them to oblige.

As if hearing Kimm's thoughts, Amick continued. "For clarification, the five billion ECs will be paid by the so-called Elites, while the confused Delegate from Lep'sor will act as a go-between for any negotiations with security personnel, the Station's management or outside representatives. He will be an obedient servant."

There was a nervous murmur in the room as understanding came to the attendees. There was no need for them to be jealous of the Lep'sorian.

"Now, if you please, I will have all the staff personnel gather to my right while the Delegates move to my left. Now, hurry. There is still much to explain."

They moved with order and quickness, anticipating that they were no longer part of the game and would soon either be released or sequestered someplace safe until this drama played out. Surely, the wealthy planets would pay the ransom in a matter of hours, and this ordeal would be over. There was almost an anxious bounce in their steps.

"Very good," Amick said. "I am glad to see you are getting into the spirit of the festivities." He stopped to survey the two groups and then the row of confident—yet irritated—Delegates in front of him. Kimm could tell the Big Five were more annoyed than scared. When it came to credits, they had no worries. Five billion was nothing to them; in fact, most had that much in personal wealth. And when compared to the wealth of their systems, there was no question the ransoms would be paid.

Kimm was relieved beyond words that he was not to be one of them. That would have meant his sure death, although, at this point in his life, death was nothing he feared. He was two weeks away from full transition no matter what happened aboard Rizen Station; even so, he preferred that his ending occur naturally and not at the hands of greedy terrorists.

"Now, I will explain more of the rules of the game. First of all, this recording is being sent to all your respective worlds, plus the ships carrying your security teams. I reiterate: They are not to attempt any rescue, otherwise it will result in your immediate execution, and by your, I mean the remaining delegates and staff. You see, you are expendable in this game, and as such, you will be used as collateral, while we seek to preserve the value of our honored guests." He waved a hand at the Big Five ... and Kimm. "But be assured, if need be, even they will be sacrificed. The game will begin in a few minutes, once instructions on how to pay the ransoms have been received on the primary worlds. And one other point, the ransoms must be unanimous. All must pay, or else all will die."

He turned his attention to the group of fifteen delegates huddled along one of the walls of the dining room. These were the expendables.

"And now for the timetable for the game." Amick grimaced. "It was regrettable that some of your colleagues didn't make the conference. Four died on the way, and two retreated. And now, after the six before me, that leaves only fifteen of you."

He nodded to a soldier near the group. He stepped over and pulled away a random Delegate.

"The game will commence at this time and will last for 14 more hours, at which point either we will have our credits or all of you will be dead."

The guard shot the delegate in the chest, avoiding the mess of an exploding skull. The others cowered and screamed, moaning as several began whimpering in their native manner.

"For every standard hour that goes by without payment, one of you will die. That leaves fourteen of you alive at this moment. If the six who failed to join us were still here, there would be more time to play the game. Regrettably, that is not the case. The good news: If payment is received within the first hour, you all shall live. If not, well, use your imagination. Oh, and another thing, any of the worlds may pay the ransoms, but it must come to us from the governments which these five individuals represent. If your governments wish to save your lives, as well as the lives of those among you, they have that right. And I will not advertise who is to be the next player to be sacrificed, so, I would begin negotiations immediately. My friend Kimm Jors will be available to receive your inquiries, although I see not why. There will be no adjustments, no bargaining, no extensions. Five billion each, twenty-five billion total. It is as simple as that."

****

Sandon Amick turned toward the camera—undoubtedly operated by one of his soldiers—and nodded. The image shifted to a stock photo of the planet Rizen, the static screen for all Station monitors.

Adam stood stunned, realizing he hadn't taken a breath in over a minute. Well, he had that figured all wrong. It wasn't the Cartels at all, but a bunch of renegade Unidor agents looking to make a quick—and sizable—score at the expense of the Conference and Unidor's reputation. Adam couldn't help but snicker. It couldn't have happened to a nicer bunch of people—those arrogant, self-righteous bastards. But now that the gloating was over, Adam was in a real predicament. There weren't one or two terrorists, but probably twenty-four, maybe more.

Then Adam shrugged. At least the company-being Endic Vor wasn't part of them. At least Adam read him right. But now the terrorists—kidnappers—whatever you wanted to call them, controlled the Station and all means on and off. Of course, Amick couldn't have expected a fly in the ointment like Adam to be wandering the halls. He amended his count—twenty-three, after subtracting for the agent he killed a few minutes ago.

Still, this was someone else's fight. Kimm seemed to be in a protected class, and Adam had no doubt the money would be paid. So, he could either just hunker down somewhere and wait for this to blow over, or he could make it to the landing bay to verify what Amick said about the lockdown was true. From his experience, that probably wasn't the case. The bad guys had to have a way off the Station, and that could be Adam's ticket to freedom.

Although he had no idea where he was, Adam did have a good sense of direction. He had to go down to the main Concourse and then aft to the landing bay. But what was aft on a wheel? He'd figure that out later. Right now, his handiwork in the suite would soon be discovered, if it hadn't already. That would let the kidnappers know that there was a rogue player in the game, although Adam had no intention of getting more involved than he already was. But Amick and his people wouldn't know that. Surely, they wouldn't leave well enough alone and not come looking for him. That was wishful thinking.

But from Adam's point of view, he said let the Bad Guys have their money. Hopefully, not too many innocent people would have to die. And as far as Kimm went, well, the Starfire contract offered no guarantees. Tidus would get paid whether Kimm made it out alive or not.

That was too bad, too. Adam liked the slimy tadpole. He was a hoot. He really hoped Kimm would make it out alive. If not, well, no bonus for Adam.

Chapter 13

Aboard the Banndock Mor cruiser, the security team was going crazy. Their leader, a Rigorian named Kalc Binn was barking orders, asking for an inventory of weapons and to ready the shuttle. That was when the CW comm sounded, and the *Manji* of Banndock Mor came on the screen.

"Kalc Binn, are you contemplating an action?" the four-eyed creature inquired.

"Yes, we are. This cannot stand. They are holding our clients." The lizard's voice was like sandpaper, and he was so angry that saliva drained from the corners of his long mouth.

"Your client is a prominent citizen of Banndock Mor, and you are to engage in *no* action that could jeopardize his welfare."

"We have over two hundred trained operatives nearby. All have clients aboard. There are but a scant few terrorists. We can affect a rescue."

"Can you guarantee no friendly casualties?" the politician asked pointedly.

"Of course not. But their leader said he will cherish the lives of the Elites above the others. That includes Hal'onkin."

"It is too much to risk. We are considering the ransom. You will do nothing until a decision is made."

Kalc was so unhinged that he couldn't control his temper. "I do not work for you!"

"And you never will again with that attitude."

The Rigorian tried to calm himself. "Forgive, but from my professional experience, if we do nothing and you pay the ransom, there is a good chance all will die anyway. And how do we know they are not ultimately working for the Cartels without regard to what their leader has said? Receiving a ransom will satisfy the Unidor soldiers, but not the Cartels. They would prefer all the Delegates to die. It will send a message to the rest of the Sector."

"It is a risk we are willing to take. Now, do as I say. Attempt no action without direct permission from Banndock Mor."

The screen went blank, and Kalc roared. The natives on the bridge trembled as the seven-foot-tall lizard stretched open his wide mouth showing all his rows of deadly teeth. "Leave the bridge!" Kalc ordered although he had no authority to issue such an order. Nevertheless, the Moreans quickly vacated the room.

The other three members of Kalc's team were on the bridge. Missing was Idera. She was not on the shuttle with the rest of the team. Perhaps she had gone with The Human. It did not matter. She was off of his team at that moment.

Kalc opened a group link with the other ships in the Delegate fleet. By then, the security teams were in charge, just as Kalc was. Everyone was talking at once, overloading the translation bugs, but each demanded action. The Rigorians were well known in the galaxy, with three of Kalc's race part of other teams. They naturally rose to leadership positions.

"We must do something," one of them managed to say through the tempest of voices.

"I agree," said a dozen more.

Kalc's head was throbbing, only adding to his frustration. He pulled his gaze from the kaleidoscope of faces on the split screen, the computer having provided enough blocks for all twenty of the other team captains. That's when he focused in on the ugly monstrosity sitting a few miles off his starboard quarter, the ship the Lep'sorians called the MOB-4.

"Silence, all of you!" Kalc yelled. "This is non-productive." The voices moderated some. "We all agree action must be taken. But we need to plan such a unified operation in person rather than through tiny boxes on a tiny screen. I suggest we convene on the Lep'sorian vessel. It is the only craft that can accommodate all of us."

There were a few calls of protest, but they quickly died away. If there were plans to be made, then let them be made. It didn't matter where.

"Leave immediately," Kalc said. "There is no time to waste."

****

Unidor Security had set up office on the B Level, among the administrative offices for the Station. It consisted of five offices and a conference room, and each of the agents, with the exception of the three top-ranking officers, shared resort rooms on C Level. Nothing fancy, but they were big enough for two people for the twelve days they would supposedly be on the Station.

The team arrived six days before the conference to survey the Station and get a lay of the land. They were given pass keys and access codes to all the systems aboard the Station and then briefed by staff on how things functioned, both from the Ladhi perspective and for the guests. There were very few foreign workers aboard Risen Station. The Ladhi used the facility as a perk for well-healed individuals and families. The pay was excellent, and the accommodations were often better than what was found on the home planet. The only aliens here were specialists—such as chefs, trainers and entertainers. Everyone else was Ladhi.

The Station had a sizeable security team of its own, but that had been replaced by Unidor for the conference. Considering the much smaller guest roster for the conference, it didn't make sense to have two massive units bumping into each other and doing redundant duties. The three-hundred-person security contingent was given the time off so they could return to their families on Ladhi.

That left only the Unidor troops with the guns aboard the Station. That was until the two hundred-plus security force for the Delegates

102

arrived. Captain Vor knew it would ruffle feathers, scales and whatever else covered those on the private security details when they were told they would have to stay aboard their vessels and not on the Station. But his second-in-command, Sandon Amick, made a great argument. Having just removed the Ladhi force, it didn't make sense to replace it with a bunch of shoddily trained loose cannons with guns, creatures that knew nothing of the operation of the Station. Besides, as has been noted, the Station would be running at less than a fifth of its normal complement of guests. The Unidor troops could handle anything that came up. That was why the Sector was hiring the company to run security for them in the first place.

The thing Captain Enrick Vor didn't realize was that the major threat to the conference was already on the Station, in the form of the team he brought aboard.

Sandon Amick—like the rest of his team—was the ultimate soldier of fortune. He spent years in the field, drifting from contract to contract even before the Klin invasion. Afterward, it became an even more target-rich environment for people like him. And then Unidor began advertising for permanent personnel, offering exorbitant salaries and willing to take anyone with military or law enforcement experience. They were anticipating huge contracts coming their way and needed to pad their numbers for their perspective clients.

Amick jumped at the opportunity to have some stability in his life. But that only lasted a few years. After that, he became restless and not satisfied with the static income he was making.

And that's when he was approached and told about the conference. The plan sounded too good to pass up. That's what the others thought, as well. After that, it was just a matter of making sure Amick and his people were on the team Captain Vor was putting together for the assignment.

Amick was a slick operator. Although skilled with all makes and models of weapons, as well as physical combat, his true talent was with the gift of persuasion. Vor didn't have a chance against his slick presentation and jumped at the chance of having such an experienced and tight-knit unit already in place and ready to go.

That was until Amick placed a Level-Two bolt into the back of his head.

"It has been confirmed," said Amick's own second-in-command, a Riilian named Ror Hazz.

"Details," Amick demanded.

Ror shook his head in disbelief. "He died from a single, close-range bolt in the chest, although there was evidence that he had been physically accosted prior to his death."

"Are we speaking of the same Bankon Kri?"

"We are. Yes, he has been one of our most effective enforcers for three years, hired for his strength and not his intelligence."

"What was he doing?"

"He was clearing Delegate's Row of service workers. We found three dead Ladhi in an elevator. Then there were signs of a struggle outside the room where Kri was found."

"Someone fought *him*?"

"Not only that, but they won, dragging Kri into a Delegate's room and tying him up. Bankon was able to call out the emergency code and location before he was killed."

"He was restrained?" Amick said, shaking his head, unbelieving. "This cannot be one of the Ladhi."

"No, it cannot. It must be one—or a team—of the bodyguards."

"They were to all leave the Station."

"That is correct. Some must have stayed."

"Who could have done this?"

Ror shook his head. "I do not know. I tend to believe it must be more than one; it is the only way Kri could have been overcome."

Amick looked through the glass window of the office he was using. It wasn't fancy, and looked out at another workspace and offices. "If they are bodyguards, then they must have seen the broadcast. They will know what they are up against."

"They will attempt to reach the landing bays to test your assertion that everything is locked down."

"Nothing this big is locked down completely."

"Perhaps we should let them escape."

Amick nodded. "Perhaps. But first, I would like to find out who they are and then kill them, if possible. If not, then you may be correct. In the meantime, our numbers are too few to have a random threat capable of taking out our troops running loose on the Station. Send out three teams of two. Have them patrol the three major Concourses. This Station is a maze of confusing hidden passageways. Even so, the easiest route to the landing bays is through the public corridors."

Amick looked at the bank of monitoring screens on the wall. His people had taken over the security department aboard the Station and had access to the camera system. He found the Ladhi to be woefully inadequate in that area, although they advertised the fact that Rizen Station was a private sanctuary for its guests, free of intrusive surveillance. What happened here would not leave the spinning ring. It was a feature they prided themselves on.

It also meant that Amick was blind to most of the Station. But he did have eyes on his special guests. The bulk of the Delegates had been moved to a large room on A Level and locked in, requiring a pair of guards to stand watch outside. Their staffs were in a nearby suite with the same security setup. The five main Delegates—the source of the massive payoff Amick and his team would soon be enjoying—were also on the A Level but being pampered with scrumptious meals prepared by hand by the few Ladhi service personnel left alive on the Station. Amick would indulge them for a while before showing his real contempt for creatures like them. Once he had the credits, he would have his fun.

Chapter 14

Adam Cain was having anything but fun. He was doing his best to make it down to the main level and found service elevators that did the trick. Originally, he thought there were only three primary levels in the Station. He was right—A, B and C. But in addition, there were something like twenty others sandwiched in between. When taking a public elevator between floors, these secondary levels were skipped, and the cars moved so fast no one noticed. But the service elevators stopped on every floor. Adam kept checking where he was at each stop, sometimes having to go out into a public corridor to get his bearings. And as each door opened, he expected to come face to face with a squad of Unidor soldiers, relieved when he didn't. The damn Station felt like a ghost town, which was fine by him

There had been nothing coming over the comm device he took from the Unidor guard in half an hour, so he was sure they knew he was here and that he had killed one of their own. They would be looking for him. But the Station was huge, and they didn't have that many troops to spare. Their *guests* had to be guarded, and other agents would be needed to monitor the intrusion systems of the Station to make sure none of the bodyguard troops attempted a rescue. Adam knew that if he were off the Station, that would be what he would be doing, planning an assault.

The thing about being lost in a spinning wheel in space was that if you kept going in the opposite direction of the spin, you would eventually end up back where you started. It was inevitable that Adam would come upon the landing bay sooner or later, and he felt more comfortable using that strategy in one of the main public corridors. He grew complacent from the lack of anyone around, letting his guard down ... until it was too late.

****

Adam had just come out of a side door onto C Concourse when an elevator pinged, and two Unidor soldiers walked out. They were skilled, with one covering the hallway in one direction while the other checked the opposite. One of them was bound to see Adam.

It was too late. A flash bolt erupted from a Xan-fi rifle, fired with reactions almost equal to Adam's. Fortunately, the creature had the same eye-to-hand coordination as most aliens and the shot missed Adam by a good ten feet.

He ducked back through the side door and sprinted down the corridor. The soldiers were in the passageway a few seconds later, and Adam could hear them yelling into their communicators with location and direction.

Although Adam had just come from the corridor, he hadn't paid much attention to where he was. The plain, grey walls all looked alike. But he couldn't stay running in a straight line; he would make a juicy target if he did.

He ducked around side hallways and eventually burst through a set of double doors into a much larger room. It was a ventilation utility shed, complete with humming equipment, spinning turbines and shiny metal ducting running along the ceiling. Throughout most of the service floors, the Ladhi hadn't bothered putting in ceiling boards, preferring to leave the wires, pipes and ducting open and accessible.

Adam ran to the other side of the room, shocked and disappointed to learn there was no secondary exit. What ventilation service center didn't have two or more exits? Apparently, this one.

He sighted along one of the main ventilation ducts, seeing an access panel about twelve feet up. The duct wasn't huge, maybe two feet in diameter. He would fit ... but not the huge aliens about to burst through the door.

Adam pulled over a service table and climbed on top. Then using the barrel of the Xan-fi, he pushed open the panel, wincing when it fell open into the duct with a loud, echoing report. If the aliens didn't know where he was before, they did now.

Adam strapped the Xan-fi over his shoulder and across his back and lined his body up under the opening. It would be a jump of about eight feet.

As a Human subjected to the often-lighter gravity of alien worlds, every chance he got, Adam would crank the internal gravity of the *Arieel* up to 125% of Earth standard just so he could get a constant workout. If not, his muscles would eventually atrophy, and he'd become just like any other alien. The strategy worked, making him not only stronger than most aliens but even stronger than the average Human.

He jumped up, easily entering the small opening with his outstretched arms and shoulders. Then he dropped his elbows, hooking himself in the duct as if his body were a grappling hook. He rolled over and pulled the rest of his body inside.

There would be no hiding where he was, but the duct disappeared in a bulkhead a few feet along the run and without a door to access the next room over. The soldiers would have to find a way to follow the duct, and by then, Adam would be long gone.

He began crawling, hearing as the guards burst into the room below. They could hear the popping and crinkling of the thin sheet metal structure of the duct, knowing where he was. But they couldn't reach the opening, and fortunately for Adam, flash bolts didn't have much penetrating power.

Still, they sent a few bolts against the overhead tubing.

Adam laughed, realizing the significance of where he was, shimmying through a dimly lit ventilation duct, being pursued by terrorists who were holding hostages, and within a secure building. He'd seen this movie before, but he refused to give into it completely. Instead, he yelled back at the aliens, hearing his words echo off the metal walls, *"Hasta la vista, yippee ki-yay!"*

He was sure the translation bugs wouldn't have a clue what he just said.

****

"He has entered a ventilation service tube," the Unidor sergeant reported. "We cannot follow."

"There is just one creature?" Amick asked.

"It is all we saw."

"I will have Loren send you a layout diagram of the ventilation system." Then the guard heard Amick snicker. "I will also send Izzi. Relay your exact position to me."

Both Unidor agents grinned at each other knowingly. *This will be fun to watch.*

Chapter 15

Adam had been in the duct for a good fifteen minutes. His elbows were bruised, and his back hurt like a bitch. He'd been blindly navigating the intricate maze of vents, looking for an exit point. So far, nothing.

The thing about air ducts is they didn't necessarily have to run horizontally. Adam came upon a number of shear shafts running up and down and disappearing into the darkness. Some did angle off not quite as severely, but they were few and far between.

Fortunately, the Xan-fi came equipped with a flashlight, so he was able to light his way. He didn't have to rely on a cigarette lighter as Bruce Willis did in *Die Hard*. And unlike John McClane, Adam wasn't too beat up. He snickered. *Not yet.*

The whirl of the air through the system, accompanied by the constant drone of circulating fans, made Adam groggy. He wondered if it might be safe to lay his head down for a while and rest. What harm would a few minutes of shut-eye cause?

He lay the side of his head against the cool metal surface of the duct, his left ear sticking to it like a suction cup.

And that was when he heard the faint scratching.

It wasn't his imagination, and Adam wondered if there were rats on the Station. It was possible, but they'd be alien rats. He shuddered at what they may look like. But the sound was getting stronger. It was uneven and not the rhythmic nature of the other noises around him. He kept his ear to the metal, unable to rest and growing more concerned by the second. Whatever it was, it was moving fast.

Adam was in a long, straight run of tubing. He rolled over and shined the light back the way he'd come. The beam disappeared into the gloom.

And then it caught a reflection, movement of some kind. Adam stared, narrowing his eyes and squinting into the vanishing light.

Then it was there; something else was in the duct and headed his way. And it was a lot larger than a rat.

Adam rolled back over and began crawling along the tube as fast as he could. Terror helped drive him as he glanced back now and then to see a larger, dark object wiggling through the duct. As it got closer—not more than twenty feet away—Adam could make out more detail.

It was a person, or more precisely, a kind of person. Sort of. It had a basic Humanoid/Prime head with shoulders and two long arms. The rest of the body was obscured by the duct. It was a lot narrower than the other Unidor guards, and then Adam noticed the features that made his skin crawl.

Projecting from the arms were dozens of shorter appendages, each covered in tiny suction cups and then capped with a single sharp, black claw. It looked to be a combination of a person and a centipede. As it drew closer, it literally slithered along the metal surface, appearing completely at home with this mode of movement. And the weirdest thing; it was wearing the Unidor colors.

Adam had never seen an alien like this before. For it to be a part of the security team, it must be able to contain the additional limbs and hold them under the uniform. It must also be intelligent and not just some chase animal sent against him. But a hundred or more half-an-inch-long claws, and the sinewy, slithering way it moved, gave Adam the chills. He was being chased by a snake/centipede/hired killer. And the damn thing could crawl a lot faster than he could.

Adam spun the Xan-fi around and fired a bolt.

The beast raised another limb, producing a clear-plastic screen known as a *Danian Shield*, a form of personal protection designed to deflect incoming flash bolts. The shield worked. And the thing kept coming.

Within seconds, it was nipping at his feet. He stopped and kicked at it, hitting the shield instead. The creature was strong, pushing back against his feet, with the tiny—yet numerous—spikes ripping at the rubber soles of his tennis shoes. Yes, Adam had opted for comfort over his heavy and more clunky combat boots. In hindsight, that may have been a mistake.

He did manage to get one good kick past the shield and into the face of the alien. It was stunned momentarily, and Adam slid away. And then it was upon him again.

Surprisingly, the creature was able to compress its body even more so it could slither on top. Adam was on his back, pressing the awkward Xan-fi between him and the creature. It smelled terrible, like the inside of a snake if you've ever cut into one. And the skin was slimy. But the Prime-like face was the incongruity that shook Adam the most. It was only inches from his ... and it was smiling.

"I have been told..." the beast grunted as it struggled with Adam, "that I get to eat you when we are done. That is good. I tire of the Station's processed food. I would prefer fresh meat."

Adam was able to press the barrel of the rifle against the smirking face. Then he closed his eyes and pulled the trigger. Even through closed eyelids, the light was blinding. But it affected the alien even more. It screamed and attempted to roll away but was jammed in with Adam's body. Adam began to crawl backward, just using his elbows and hips. He couldn't see where he was going, so it came as a surprise when he and the centipede tumbled over the edge of a downward-sloping side vent.

This shaft was about twice the size of the vents Adam had been in, allowing the pair to tumble over and around each other, each trying to find purchase against the smooth metal walls. Even though the beast wasn't attacking, the prickly spikes tore at Adam's shirt and skin, shredding the former and puncturing the latter. The presence of warm, slick blood only added to their downward plunge.

Adam glanced downward during one of the uncontrollable rolls the pair was making, catching a glimpse of a flashing light. From his experience in the ventilation system, he knew this to be a circulating fan, which was nothing more than a series of sharp, spinning blades placed right in the middle of the shaft.

Adam tugged at the beast, cutting his hand on the myriad of sharp spikes, pushing the creature past him and facing the oncoming blades. The alien saw what was coming and struggled to change places with Adam.

It almost made it.

The blades jerked to a stop as several of them dug into soft flesh before reaching the more stubborn bone. Blood was everywhere, and the whining of the jammed motor harmonized with the whimpering of the rapidly dying alien.

The blades continued to press against the corpse, digging ever more into the bloody mess. They wouldn't hold for long.

Adam was sitting atop the dead alien. Now he kicked at the blades, which only served to free them up to spin a little more. He kicked again, seeing one of the blades bend, opening a little more space between the next. A third kick was enough for Adam to dive through.

Unfortunately, the Xan-fi fell through before him and became stuck blocking his way, leaving him half in the circle of deadly blades and half out. He tugged at the weapon, only lodging it against a side junction box even more. Panicking, Adam began to hammer at the blades with his fists. The fans were sharp but not that thick. They began to deform. They also began to spin.

Adam tucked his legs inward, and for a moment, he was wrapped around the inner bearings of the spinning wheel. He spun with it as the blades became freer, allowing the motor to pick up speed. His vision was a blur, his mind disoriented and with the centrifugal force about to throw him outward.

Then a blade came free, whirling by only inches from his head, before it impaled itself in a side wall. The rest of the fan began to come apart, sending three-foot-long razor-sharp metal blades shooting off in all directions.

Adam's bloody arms held on to the central wheel with all their might, letting the blades—one or two at a time—fly off. Finally, there were no more blades, and the wheel mercifully wound to a stop.

Adam continued to hold on, and for good reason. For one, the fan was set at the midpoint in the tunnel and not the bottom. He still had a ways to fall. And second, there was blood, bone and sinew everywhere. He had to be careful where he stepped or placed a hand.

Even though he didn't feel pain like a normal person and would heal quicker, the psychological trauma he'd just experienced would take some time to get over. Although there wasn't a lot of the centipede-like thing left, the memory would haunt him for years. He'd seen some weird shit in his time ... *but damn.*

Shaking his head to reset his determination, he looked down at where he had to go next. The angled shaft was larger than the smaller, horizontal duct, he'd been in before. The fan was set at a point with struts and electronics attached to the wall. The Xan-fi rifle was hung up on a junction box.

He checked his body. Except for dozens of tiny puncture wounds, he was in relatively good shape. It looked worse than it was. His shirt was soaked in blood and essentially useless, but he still had the MK tucked in his pants, a miracle of miracles.

Resolving himself to another difficult climb down the shaft, Adam untangled himself from the center hub of the now-dead fan and braced his rubber soles against one side of the shaft with his back pressed against the others side. He cradled the Xan-fi in his lap and began to slowly move down the vent.

It worked ... for about twenty feet until the blood-soaked shirt caused his back to slip, and he lost his purchase, falling back down the shaft.

He sprawled out on the angled surface and spread his legs. The soles of his shoes squeaked and slipped until they eventually began to slow his fall using a technique mountain climbers call *stemming*. Even after he stopped the descent, it took him a while to get the courage to move his feet. Six inches and one shoe at a time, he began to move again.

To his relief, he didn't have to go all the way to the bottom, wherever that was. He came to a horizontal side duct and ingloriously tumbled into it and lay on his back, panting. He stayed there for a full ten minutes before rolling over and crawling along the tunnel.

He didn't go far before coming to an end grate that fed air into the room below. It was a storage room, full of linen and other bedding.

Adam kicked out the grate and struggled over the edge, letting himself fall to the floor in the light gravity. Even then, it was a jolt when he hit the deck and then managed to stand. It seemed like days since he last stood up. It hurt.

He moved to a stack of towels and, after removing what was left of his shirt, he began to wipe the still moist blood from his body, from all over his body. Fortunately, the puncture wounds were like pinpricks, and they were already closing up as his body continued the slow-motion cloning process. For good measure, he tucked a couple of extra hand towels in his waistline and then went to the door.

He had no idea where he was except that he had to be below C Concourse and probably close to the inner hull of the ring-shaped Station. The landing bay was on Level C, but where along the floor, he wasn't sure. He'd made his way back there after the one and only visit he made to Kimm's suite, but those were different times. He wasn't under stress, and it still took half an hour to get there.

He moved among the spiderweb of hidden passageways until he came to an elevator, a service elevator. He cringed at the possibility of being trapped in the carnival ride again, not knowing where he would end up. But fuck it. He was tired and frustrated and just wanted to get somewhere familiar, even if a squad of Unidor agents would be waiting for him. They had to figure he'd head for the landing bay ... unless he intended to take on the whole Unidor force by himself. Adam laughed aloud. He was stupid, but not *that* stupid.

He entered the elevator, and the sensor closed the door and set the car in motion. As usual, Adam had the Xan-fi rifle ready when the door opened.

Chapter 16

Fortunately, no one was there, and the car opened to one of the main Levels, one with plush carpeting and side decorations along the wall. Adam recognized it as the C Concourse. Looking both ways, he recognized even more. There were doorways and opened portals, including one that led to the reception hall where he and the other bodyguards once mingled. For a brief moment, he thought of Idera and was glad she wasn't trapped aboard this nightmare of a Station like he was. What he wouldn't give to be sitting with her right now, enjoying a fruity intoxicant and making simple conversation about their adventures among the stars. Maybe someday ... if he could get off this rust bucket.

Adam began to make his way toward the landing bay, confident he knew where he was going. But he had to be careful. Although most of the Unidor agents might think he was dead, killed by their weird teammate, they might still have troops stationed at the landing bay.

He moved up to the main Concourse, where arriving guests got their first impression of Rizen Station. There were now deserted shops and small eateries lining the corridor with signage that was written in Ladhi, but that was also linked to translation bugs as Adam walked by. Without his permission, barkers were trying to sell him everything from watches to suppositories—he figured that had to be a thing in some alien cultures. But soon, he was past the commercial district and into the main hangar.

There were seven separate receiving and departing bays, each with their pairs of airlocks capable of handling anything smaller than a Juirean Class-3. Since none of the bodyguard ships were here, and all the other guests were off the station, the chambers were relatively empty except for a fleet of a dozen mid-range shuttles. These had been used to ferry the mercs back to their ships and had a range that would take them from Rizen Station all the way to Ladhi. Adam was just about to sprint over to the nearest one to see if they really were locked down, as that asshole on the broadcast had said. Until he heard a voice; it was vaguely familiar.

Crouching along the side bulkhead in Bay C, he moved closer to the sound. It was a single person talking. He could have been talking to another person in the room or over a comm device.

Glancing around the forward section of a shuttle, Adam saw two people walking side by side. One was a Unidor agent, his Xan-fi held casually across his chest. The other was Kimm Jors, his client.

Adam quickly ducked back under cover. He didn't want to risk alerting the agent and getting Kimm killed in the process. The last he'd seen of Kimm, he was on the broadcast and being assigned go-between duties by the terrorist leader, some asshole named Sandon Amick. Go-between for whom was still a question. The parties involved in the ransom negotiations would be light-years away. Adam couldn't see what part Kimm would play.

But it was obvious he was here under guard. One armed agent was enough to secure the pacifistic tadpole. Adam could use that to his advantage.

He slipped back along the port side of the shuttle so he could come up from behind. He didn't know if there were other agents in the landing bay, so he preferred not to use his weapons. His hands would be his weapons.

There was plenty of cover as he approached, moving between crates, storage barrels and charging stations. The pair was walking along slowly, and Adam's tennis shoes helped to keep the sound of his footsteps to a minimum.

When he was about ten feet behind, he rushed forward. He had to leave his feet to jump high enough to wrap his right forearm around the neck of the alien, locking it in place with his left. The creature reacted by clawing at Adam's arms, but the Human wasn't playing around.

Once his feet touched the floor again, he braced himself and twisted, snapping the alien's neck.

Adam violently tossed the body aside with an emphatic, "Fuck you!"

Kimm had backed away from the twenty-second attack, standing at a distance with his mouth agape. The black orbs for eyes seemed to have grown by about twenty-five percent.

And that wasn't all. Adam was shocked to see that Kimm's hunchback was nearly double the size of the last time he saw him, and that was only a couple of hours ago. Did the transition cause such drastic changes so quickly?

"Kimm, what the hell are you doing here?"

At first, the Lep'sorian was too shocked to speak. He looked at the dead guard and then back at Adam, seemingly more frightened of Adam than he had been of the Unidor soldier.

"Adam Cain? Is that you?"

Adam had to admit he looked a sight. His chest and arms were bare, with most of the exposed skin covered in tiny red dots, making him look as if he had the measles, if aliens would even know what measles were.

"Yeah, it's me. Boy, am I glad to see you. I saw you in the broadcast; are you okay?"

"Yes, I am perfectly well."

It sounded like an accusation. Adam had seen Kimm like this before, after the attack of the MOB-4 by the Cartel ships. At the time, Adam chalked it up to the stress of the attack and the chemical changes the Lep'sorian's body had to be going through. Seeing all that had happened recently on the Station, he could be going through the same thing again.

"That's good. Now come along. I want to see if I can get any of these ships going. We need to get out of here—"

"But I am not leaving!"

There was that arrogant, defiant voice again. *He's definitely going through some changes,* Adam thought.

"What do you mean you're not going?"

"I have been made a vital part of the drama that is unfolding. I cannot abandon my fellow Delegates."

"You mean that bunch of obnoxious, self-righteous assholes who have been laughing at you all day? You don't owe them anything."

"But you are wrong. Besides, two of my staff still survive. I cannot abandon them."

"The ransom will probably be paid, no matter what you do. Everyone should be okay."

"And if I escape? How will Sandon Amick react to that? Will he kill my staff, along with additional Delegates not of the Elites?"

Kimm had a point. Amick might do all that, and more.

Adam shook his head.

"I don't have time for this. I'm being hunted, and I can't hang around. I'm getting off the Station. This isn't my fight; it's between people with money against those who want to take it from them. You can come if you want, but I'm leaving."

"If you are able."

"If I'm able, yeah, sure. Are you coming or not?"

"I am not."

Adam pursed his lips in frustration. "Well, then, it's been nice knowing you. I hope everything works out. Now, get out of here. Go back to your Delegate friends before you're missed."

"And what about him?" Kimm said indicating the body at their feet.

"It will take a while before they find him. I'll be long gone by then. Just don't say anything for as long as you can. Give me time to get away."

"I will do that."

"Thanks." Adam reached out a hand to shake, something Kimm had done when they first met. Now the alien looked at him as if he'd just farted.

Adam shrugged it off again to the transmutation the tadpole was going through. No telling what hormones were raging in that confused and obscenely shaped body.

Adam nodded and then rushed off into the bay. Kimm hurried off in the opposite direction, wanting to get as far away from The Human as he could. Mentally, Adam wished him luck. He would need it.

And so would Adam.

Chapter 17

The first shuttle Adam checked was locked up tighter than a drum, as was the second and the third. There were other ships in the bay, and he rushed over to them.

There were four smaller jump ships, each painted in the dark green and black of Unidor colors. These would be the getaway ships for the terrorists, plus a vessel for the executive who had been killed earlier. They wouldn't be locked down.

But they were *locked*.

Adam checked the code pad. It was setup for a pass card. Adam quickly tried the universal pass key he had for the Station. It didn't work.

Desperately, he jumped onto a stubby wing of the starship and scanned the landing bay, looking for any other options for getting off the Station. The action saved his life.

He saw the three Unidor soldiers enter the chamber, Xan-fis gripped and moving in attack formation. This wasn't a random patrol; they were here looking for him. But how did they know he was here? Did Kimm tell them? He could have, hoping to gain favor with the terrorists.

Unfortunately, the agents saw Adam at the same time he saw them. They were coming in from the port side of the starship, so Adam dove over the cockpit to his right, sliding along the smooth glass canopy and the cold, slippery metal, metal that burned the bare skin of his chest as he slid across. He was up on the opposite wing as flash bolts zinged overhead.

The Unidor soldiers were well-trained—for aliens. They moved closer to the starship, one covering while two of them sprinted to new cover. Adam slid off the wing to the deck, being careful to stay hidden by the ship's extended landing pads. He raced off toward the next ship, sliding on his hip under the vessel.

Here he rolled over on to his belly, taking the Xan-fi and sighting it under the starship and across the room. He could see the Unidor agents, but they were a good hundred yards away. Xan-fis were made for long-distance, but long distance by alien standards. This was just about at the weapon's maximum range. Energy bolts lost integrity down range, so Adam cranked the Level up to One. With the rifle, this would give him ten shots. The range didn't change, it just meant that if he hit anything, the bolt would count.

He sighted a soldier. He only had a narrow shot, so he set two of them off in rapid succession, hoping to saturate the target area.

It worked. The first bolt hit the agent in the shoulder, burning a hole in his uniform and spinning him around. The second bolt caught him in the neck a split second later.

Another disadvantage of using an energy weapon was the bolts were so bright and moved at such speed that they looked more like beams rather than single balls of plasma. The beams allowed the enemy to instantly identify the source of the incoming fire, and the agents sent off a dozen Level-2 panic shots in his direction.

Adam covered his head with his arms, overcome by the intense light and heat from the bolts striking around him. He was under the cover of a landing strut, but that hardly mattered. Burning heat still reached his bare skin.

"Jesus Christ!" Adam groaned, his face contorted in pain and anguish.

Fortunately, there came a reprieve as the two agents drained their battery packs of Level-2 bolts and had to stop to snap in new cartridges. Unfortunately, they seemed to have come fully stocked with replacements.

Adam was up and sprinting away as the second continuous barrage of incoming bolts splattered around him. He jumped in the light gravity, flying over a row of barrels before landing hard against the metal deck and crashing into another bulkhead. He was safe for the moment. Until he noticed the barrels were marked with the universal symbol for lifting fuel, the chemical propellant used in takeoff and landing jets. And it was highly combustible.

The Unidor agents didn't seem to care. They'd followed his run and were now sending star-hot white balls of plasma energy striking the tough metal barrels. They were designed to withstand considerable abuse before exploding, but Adam didn't want to take the chance they would reach their limit with him only a few feet away.

He set off along the bulkhead, exposing himself to clear fire, but being aliens, they were relying on the number of shots aimed at their target rather than accuracy. The white balls would hit the bulkhead and then spread out in a splashing motion, expanding their reach. Adam dodged and ducked, covering his head with his hands and the Xan-fi.

He aimed the weapon behind him and opened fire. Even shooting backward, he was more accurate than the aliens. He stopped firing as he dived for cover.

Adam was out of Landing Bay 3 a moment later, sprinting along the outer receiving concourse and past Bay 4. He found a clear stretch of the hallway without any cover and stopped at the other side, sliding around a corner and then laying on his stomach again, ready to fire at anything that came down the Concourse.

The agents came, but they were cautious. One stayed back, his weapon pointed down the corridor, while the other slinked along the wall, his weapon also at the ready.

Adam's finger was on the trigger. This would be where he demonstrated the difference between Humans and aliens.

He aimed the barrel around the corner and, in a split second, had already sighted and released two bolts, one going about forty feet and the other fifty. Both were on target, hitting the agents, one center mass on the agent along the wall and the other in the leg of the covering alien.

Adam was up a second later. The soldier hit in the leg wasn't dead, but he was momentarily distracted by his injury. By the time he came to his senses and attempted to lift his weapon, Adam was upon him, pumping two more bolts into his body. At this range—and firing at Level-1—it wasn't pretty.

Adam surveyed his handiwork, feeling no remorse for his enemy. Then he dropped the power pack from his Xan-fi and snapped in an extra he'd taken off the first agent he killed. Then he collected two more packs from the body at his feet.

Unless Amick sent additional troops, Adam was in the clear, at least for a while. He made a quick mental tally. He'd killed six of the terrorists so far. He didn't know for sure how many there were to start with, but the number of twenty-four was a good guess. That still left eighteen of the bastards on the Station. That was too much. He'd pressed his luck far enough already. All it would take would be a lucky hit by some cross-eyed alien, and that would be it. And after all Adam Cain had been through in his life—both of them—he wasn't about to let it end here.

However, he still had the problem of *how* to get off the Station.

Then somewhere in his mind's eye, he remembered seeing something during his headlong flight away from the tempest of incoming flash bolts. He backtracked, reentering Bay 3.

There they were—a set of three bulky maintenance MMVs. Of course, they wouldn't be called *Manned* Maintenance Vehicles, but it was close enough. They were spacesuits fitted with jet packs and additional oxygen, along with a pair of articulated arms and grippers that workers used outside the Station. There was also an access airlock nearby.

Adam rushed to the door and checked the controls. They were still active; after all, there was no need to keep someone from leaving the Station via a single airlock. Where would they go ... outside? Into space?

But Adam knew exactly where he'd go. There was a small fleet of Delegate starships sitting only a couple of hundred miles from Rizen Station. That may sound like a long way, but these spacesuit units were designed for extended time outside the Station, working on regular and emergency maintenance. With luck, his air would hold out until he reached one of the ships, the largest, of course, being the MOB-4. All he had to do was give the unit a good burst of speed, and he would coast the rest of the way over, needing only a strong second burst to slow down.

Adam's heart pounded with excitement—and relief—as he opened the front plate of the nearest suit and climbed in. This was going to work. Soon he'd be off the Station and headed to friendlier company—well, relatively friendlier. At least the Indies weren't trying to kill him.

Screw Rizen Station. As he'd told Kimm, this wasn't his war. Let the powers that be fight over the credits. Adam Cain was outta here.

****

Adam had never flown an MMV before, but it wasn't that hard to learn.

After climbing in and sealing the suit, he checked the O2 supply and propellant charge. Both were full. Then he spent a few minutes trying to decipher the operating controls. They were simple. But then he wondered how does he get this two-ton contraption into the air lock and out into space?

Glancing up, he saw a rail line, with large grippers dangling down. He followed the track, seeing that it entered the airlock. So, a track to launch and recover the MMV. Cool. But how did he activate the rail line?

After trial and error—and another ten minutes wasted—Adam found the controls to the rail system below him on his right. A simple press of a button and the system activated itself, dropping the hook that attached to a loop on top of the suit. The unit was lifted and moved smoothly to the airlock.

Adam kept looking around, expecting at any minute to see more Unidor troops rush into the chamber. There was a spinning light and warning klaxon sounding, which would alert anyone in the area where he was. It had been over twenty minutes since he killed his last agent. Surely, someone would be calling to find out what happened. When no answer came through, reinforcements would be sent.

And the damn rail system was moving like molasses in winter.

But soon, he was in the airlock. The rail stopped as the chamber sealed up and evacuated the atmosphere. The unit was placed outside and released, leaving Adam was momentarily stunned by the awesome sight outside the Station. He was on the Rizen side of the resort, getting the full scope of the size, the colors and the wonder that was the double-ringed planet. And it was bright, reflecting the distant Ladhi sun off its kaleidoscope of swirling red, yellow and black clouds on the surface.

But Adam didn't have time to be a tourist. He was outside the Station and slowly moving in sync with the massive spinning ring, being drawn back to the hull by the enveloping influence of the internal gravity wells. He gave a quick burst of the reactive jets to put a little distance between himself and the hull. This close, the curving exterior of the Station looked more like a straight wall. He couldn't see the top or the bottom. He moved farther away to get his bearings.

He was on the planetside of the Station, which meant he had to get to the other side to line up with the fleet. He played with the controls, happy to learn that they were self-correcting, keeping him from putting the MMV into an uncontrollable spin. After a few minutes, he was far enough away that he could take in the entire Station through the faceplate.

He spun the unit around, scanning in the distance for any sign of the Delegate fleet. Two hundred miles was a long way, but not in space.

He saw a tiny reflection of the Ladhi sun off a shiny surface. Around it was a few smaller reflections. They weren't stars; this was the MOB-4 and a few of the larger Delegate ships. He had his target. He lined up the best he could, checked his propellant level and O2, and then hit the gas. There was a moment of gravity pressing against his chest as he accelerated. But once at speed, he fell back into weightlessness. He would have time and propellant to make midcourse corrections, so he wasn't worried that he'd be off target a little.

He had no way of deciphering the Ladhi monitors on the heads-up display before him, so he had no idea how fast he was going. All he knew was that he was off the damn Station and heading for safety. He relaxed, even contemplating a short nap. But without a way to wake him up, he didn't risk it. Instead, he focused on the brightest spot in the distance—the MOB-4. He would be there in an hour or two, maybe less.

Chapter 18

Kalc Binn swung his long snout around the room, seeing the harping gaggle of mercenary bodyguards filling the huge room. His idea to have all the independents meet on the Lep'sorian ship was a good one; the vessel could easily accommodate all two-hundred-plus mercs. But having them all in one room didn't do much to solve his problem. They were all talking at once, each wanting to be in charge, and insisting on a dozen separate plans designed to save their client, and not much more. But Kalc was after more.

He had the room's only microphone and used it to his advantage. His thick voice boomed, echoing off the metal walls of what had obstensibly been designed as a massive dining room in proportion to the other dimensions of the gawdy vessel.

"Silence! This is getting us nowhere."

If for no other reason than to get the huge lizard to dial back on the volume, many in the room fell silent.

"That is better. Now, do not misunderstand my intentions. I am not insisting on leading the operation. All I want to do is make a few points." Now the room was completely silent. Knowing that the Rigorian wasn't going to press to be the leader, many of the others calmed down.

"First, we have an incredible opportunity here. The Unidor scum have lost much today, when their own elements have turned into the enemy, and this only days before the company was to take over all security within the Sector. They will have trouble recovering from this. And you, my brothers, can take advantage of this by rescuing the hostages—all of them. Think what it will do for our companies and our reputations. Soon, we were to be placed under the foot of Unidor soldiers. Now we can put them under ours."

The enthusiastic cheers were universal. No one disputed the truth of Kalc's words.

"But first, my fellow Indies, we must have a comprehensive plan for assaulting the Station. We must be unified and in agreement with what action we take." He looked out at the myriad of alien faces looking at him. He grinned, the corners of his long mouth showing glistening long teeth. "We are an army, an army of mercenaries. This Sandon Amick worm has but a fraction of our numbers and little of our skill, and he must guard a Station that is one of the largest in the galaxy. He cannot do it. There are weaknesses, and we must find them."

"We have not much time," said a voice in the audience. "They will kill a client every standard hour. They have already killed two, with another coming soon. A plan must be developed quickly."

"I agree, and that is why I suggest we break into four teams of approximately fifty. Each team will devise a plan, after which the group as a whole will decide on which is the most viable. But only four. We cannot have twenty separate plans and expect to save anyone. As you said, we will run out of time ... and clients."

He laughed, as did others. To the mercs, this was more of a game than a desperate act of life or death. They had done their jobs and delivered their clients safely to the conference. What happened during the conference was beyond their scope of responsibility. They could stay aboard their ships and do nothing, and their companies would be paid and with no reputations harmed. They knew it. This was just a way of impressing the Sector and beyond. News of the rescue would spread across the galaxy. And Kalc was expecting his name to read prominently in the reports.

Of course, there was already one among them who could steal the spotlight from Kalc. He had that reputation. However, Kalc could not remember seeing him in the room or anywhere else on the ship. And this was his transport vessel.

Kalc lifted the microphone again and asked the assembled mercenaries, "Where is The Human?"

****

The Human could clearly see the MOB-4. Of course, in space, distances were deceptive. The ship was more than a dot of light by now; it was now an oblong dot of light. But he could also see the other twenty vessels plus the assorted escort fighters that some of the wealthier worlds provided for their representatives. Another fifteen minutes and he could start decelerating.

And damn, he was ready. It had taken two hours to travel the distance. He was tired, beat up, hungry and really had to take a piss. He was pretty sure the suit had the means of capturing his waste, but he didn't want to take the chance if he were wrong. Besides, the proportions may be off. The suit was built for the much larger Ladhi, and Adam had trouble staying in the seat, drifting instead around in the semi-spacious cockpit.

So far, he was doing fine on fuel and oxygen. Another fifteen to twenty minutes wouldn't be a problem.

****

Kalc was surprised when a huge side monitor came on within the dining area. The mercs were in four separate parts of the room, huddled together in noisy groups of twenty-five. It was still hard to hear, but within each group, it was tolerable.

Kalc's team consisted of some of his closest merc friends plus his San'nor team—minus the midget Idera. She apparently had decided to stay aboard the other transport vessel and sulk. That was fine. She mostly got in his away. His group was making progress on a plan involving entry through the observation station at the top of the ring. The Ladhi allowed for excursions outside the Station on long tethers so that guests could see the planet Rizen in all its wondrous splendor. There were small airlocks surrounding the observation pod.

But now all eyes turned to the screen. It was filled with the Rizen Station logo but was soon replaced with the smirking and confident face of the alien Sandon Amick.

"Please allow for two-way visuals," he said politely.

All eyes now turned to Kalc. It was satisfying; they saw him as their default leader, just as he hoped.

"Do not fear the revelation of any secrets," said Amick. "I know all the Independents are aboard the Lep'sorian ship, undoubtedly planning an assault on the Station. I wish to discuss terms."

Kalc nodded to a Lep'sorian crewmember near the screen. He worked the controls, and an inset image appeared in the corner of the screen showing a close-up of Kalc. That was good. It didn't reveal the true number of mercs in the room.

"I am Kalc Binn. I speak for the Independents."

"Greetings, Kalc Binn. To refresh your memory, I am Sandon Amick—"

"I know who you are."

"Good, then you must have some idea why I have made this link. I wish to caution you and the others about any attempt to enter the Station. I do not wish to engage the Indies in combat. All we are here for are the credits the Delegates can surely afford. Already, we have had contact with the relevant parties and negotiations are underway. There is no need for you to interfere at this point. Soon, your clients—"

"Will be dead!" someone in the audience yelled. "You have already killed two."

"And I will soon kill another," Amick said unabashedly. "Those are the rules of the game. But in the end, we will be paid, and many of your clients will be freed."

"Sandon Amick," Kalc began. "I appreciate that some Delegates *may* survive, but they will do so only because you allow it. You are leaving the rest of us—the ones hired to protect them—with no say in this game of yours."

"That is true, but what else can I do? Your pending action was expected, as was your migration to the Lep'sorian ship. All I am doing is pleading for restraint. There is no need for either of us to have conflict in this matter. Sit it out, live another day, and once this is done, if you wish to pursue my team and me, you will have that right."

"And that we will!" came another voice from within the room.

"Regrettably, that is something I also predict. Kalc Binn, I ask you directly, will you promise no action against the station?"

"You have heard the others. There is something to be said for being Indies. We will vote, but I believe you already know the outcome."

Amick nodded, his face a study in anguish and regret. "You are correct. Again, regrettably. Then I say goodbye. You must give me credit for trying."

"I give you credit for nothing!" Kalc bellowed, but already Amick had cut the link.

****

Adam was getting closer. He rubbed the control stick, readying for a blast of gas that would begin to slow the MMV. Considering the time he'd traveled and distance, he had to be going around a hundred miles per hour. Of course, to him, he had no sensation of movement. It was as if the tiny fleet of Delegate vessels was slowly approaching him.

And then there was the briefest of flashes coming from the MOB-4 ... and then the vessel began to fly apart. Adam stared mesmerized at what he saw, hoping it was just an illusion, a trick the light from the Ladhi star was playing on the starship.

It was no illusion.

Explosions in space didn't come with spectacular fireballs. That would require oxygen. Instead, pieces just separated and began tumbling through space at incredible speed.

Adam was still many miles away, but already he could see huge sections of superstructure headed his way.

"What the fuck?" he cried out in the cockpit of the MMV. *The damn thing just exploded!* And he was headed straight into the maelstrom.

Adam steered the MMV to the right, heading for the cluster of other Delegate vessels nearby. A few had been consumed by the explosion, feeling the invisible shock wave or being ripped apart by shrapnel raining out from the much larger ship. For Adam, it could take several seconds for some of the faster-moving pieces to reach him. He gunned the jets before changing course as a tumbling section of twisted metal passed before him. He pulled back on the throttle and cranked the controls to the left. More pieces of the MOB-4 reached him. He didn't have radar to track the chunks; everything had to be done by sight. And now that the jagged pieces didn't reflect starlight as much, they were almost impossible to see until they were right on top of him.

Soon the rain of debris lessened. Adam could still see the remains of the starship. A large section had blown out, but not the entire ship. It was a given that no one survived the explosion, but that meant Adam didn't have to dodge an unlimited supply of incoming shrapnel. He was also closer to the other ships in the fleet. Still, he wondered what else could go wrong today.

His answer came a few seconds later when all the remaining Delegate ships bolted away, first on chemical ramjets before disappearing in gravity-wells a few minutes later. Fortunately, none of them lit off in his direction. Otherwise, Adam might be seeing the inside of a gravity-well from, well, the inside.

But then reality hit him. The carcass of the MOB-4 was invisible by now, and all he could see around him was ... nothing. All the Delegate ships were gone and he was alone, drifting in space, with nowhere to go. He checked his fuel. It was less than half. And his oxygen was about the same.

He activated a light burst of the jets and spun the MMV around. Before him lay the brilliant double-ringed world of Rizen. And clearly visible, even at this distance, was Rizen Station.

With a deep sigh of resignation, Adam blasted a jet of gas that sent him off again, this time toward the Station. It would be a miracle if he made it back. He couldn't gun the jets to get there quicker because he wouldn't have the propellant to slow down. And he couldn't take his time getting back because he would run out of oxygen. It would be a fine balance between time, fuel and oxygen.

And then once he got back, he couldn't reenter the Station the same way he left. The ten minutes or more being recovered by the rail system would surely set off alarms, with a lot of pissed off Unidor soldiers waiting for him when the airlock opened.

He would need time to find another way in ... if there was one. And he needed the fuel and oxygen to find out.

"Jeez," Adams said aloud. "They don't pay me enough for this crap. Not even close."

Chapter 19

"It is done," Sandon Amick half whispered under his breath. His second in command, Ror Hazz nodded.

"You had no choice; they left you with none."

"Still, these were fellow Indies. They were not being paid to all die without honor."

"It was predicted. There could not be so many mercs in one area and not expect an operation to be planned."

Amick was finished with this part of the conversation. He shrugged. What was done was done. Now he moved to the next topic.

"Are we sure The Human left the station?"

"There was a maintenance suit missing, and the time record on the airlock confirms someone went out. We have searched the landing bay, and he is nowhere to be found. Perhaps he was aboard the Lep'sorian ship."

"That is a possibility." Amick slammed his fist on the desk. "I have lost six teammates. We only have eighteen left, and we still have beings that require guarding. And this is beyond the Delegates and their staff. There is still around a hundred Ladhi workers onboard."

"Perhaps we should eliminate the need to guard them."

"The workers?"

"Yes."

Amick thought on that for a moment before nodding. "Do it discretely so as to not cause a riot among the walking dead."

"Very well."

"And the charges?"

"They have all been set."

"Good," said Amick. "Our Cartel friends will appreciate the gesture, one given without charge. And the detonator?"

"He has it."

"Again, excellent. Now all we must wait for are the credits."

"They are beginning to come in," Ror announced. "Deposits have been made by two of the five."

"The delay with the others?"

"It seems our Tel'oran friends have found that the worlds represented by the minor Delegates are more willing to part with a few credits if it means getting their people back. The Tel'orans are holding out to see how much of the shortage they will have to pay. Others are following their example. And the more Delegates we kill, the more the survivors are willing to pay."

"And that is why the Tel'orans have the richest economy in the Sector. Keep track of the credits. It should not be too much longer."

****

Adam was sucking fumes—both literally and figuratively—by the time he made it back to the Station. He was breathing shallow and had just about used up the last of his propellant just getting the MMV down to a respectable speed. Still, it was too fast for a gentle docking. He would have to do something a little more drastic.

He had time to think about it on the way back to the Station and decided to use the internal gravity pods to help slow him down. The Station was set up on a single plane, with a top and a bottom. Below the Station extended eighteen five-mile-long rods with gravity generators on their ends. These generators produced limited-range gravity bubbles that overlapped and extended the full height of the Station, providing the internal gravity. If one was to measure it, it would be found that the gravity on Level A was slightly less than that on Level C, but not enough to notice. But this meant there were gravity-wells that Adam might be able to use to slow down the MMV.

He tried to map out the vector he would use on the way back to the Station. He was pretty sure it would work—or else he would crash into the Station and be smashed like a pancake, or he'd be sucked into the singularity. Just a typical day at the office for *The Human*, Adam Cain.

He wished he'd stop talking about himself in the third person. He was right here. He could hear everything he was thinking.

He steered the MMV under the Station and began angling toward the area just below the gravity generators and heading toward the ship. The series of microscopic black holes were created below the generators, so coming in from this angle meant he would be drawn down, away from the Station and therefore be slowed. But the balance had to be right.

He felt the tug of gravity almost immediately, sensing the influence of the well. He slowed markedly and then continued to slow; in fact, he had to gun the jets a little to keep moving toward the Station. He got to the hull and began moving up, looking for any access point he could find. He also had an idea where to find it.

It was the loading ports for the Station's food supply. A venue this big required a lot of food, including general paste stock for the processors, but also the real stuff for the high-roller guests. These shipments would be constant and brought in through a separate bay other than the one paying guests used. Adam had a good idea where the kitchen was from his adventures in the maze of internal passageways. He just needed to find the service bays.

They weren't hard to find. There were landing bays with markings and words on the hull, all written in Ladhi. There were six wide, rectangular seams on the surface of the Station, indicating service bays, although they were all closed at the time. Adam steered the MMV along the surface, looking for control panels.

It was strange having gravity outside the Station, but that's what he had. The MMV and everything around it was subject to the same draw from the gravity-wells as were the people inside the Station. This required Adam to keep a steady thrust going in order to keep from being pulled down into the well.

And then the jets sputtered and cut out.

Adam reached out with the articulated arms of the MMV, trying to grab hold of anything he could find on the hull. There were plenty of objects jutting from the surface of the Station, but he missed them all. He was sliding along, gaining speed. He then curved the pincher tines so they formed a hook and let them scrape along the metal hull.

Suddenly, Adam was jerked to a stop, causing a whiplash that sent a spasm of pain down his spine. He let the sensation pass before moving. The claw was hooked on a solid metal bar, but barely. When he shifted in the suit, he saw the metal fingers begin to slip toward the end.

Panicking, Adam pressed the emergency release button that would jettison the now useless jet pack along with the articulated arms. Adam was flung out of the seat, still in the suit but with only a small reserve air bladder to keep him alive. He grabbed handholds on the hull with his gloved hands and began to pull himself up.

He worked his way up to the nearest control panel. It was like climbing a rope ladder as he fought against the tug of gravity. But the force was stronger here than it was farther up the hull, but still less than Earth normal.

Adam still couldn't read Ladhi, but he knew airlocks. He worked the controls and lights began to flash telling him something was happening.

A large section of the hull nearby began to open. It was large enough to handle one of the midrange shuttles, the vessels used to bring food and other supplies to the Station from the planet.

He made his way over to the opening, crawling inside before working his way to the other side and another set of controls. He worked the airlock controls before the door had fully opened, closing it again.

Pressurization was done automatically and a couple of minutes later, Adam moved through a smaller airlock door and back into Rizen Station. He took off the helmet and announced—to no one in particular—"Honey, I'm home."

He stripped off the spacesuit, leaving him bare chested once again. Miraculously, he still had the MK, although he'd left the Xan-fi back in the main landing bay.

He looked around.

"Now that I'm here, what do I do?"

Chapter 20

He began walking. Since he was close to the kitchen, the first thought that came to mind was to get something to eat. He hadn't eaten in hours except for some cardboard faux hamburger at the bodyguard's dinner. He was famished.

He began to pass through workstations and past giant freezers, along with industrial-sized food processors now sitting idle. What he was looking for was something that was thawed. So far, no luck.

Then he heard the distinctive sound of flash bolts going off nearby.

He pulled the MK-17 and instinctively checked the battery pack. It was full. He also had two extra battery packs should he need them. He dialed it to Level-2.

He moved through the room before stopping to do a quick look-see around the corner. What he saw made his blood freeze.

It was a pile of dead Ladhi workers, and a Unidor soldier was throwing more bodies onto the stack. There had to be thirty or more in the pile. Adam gnashed his teeth and lifted the MK.

But then the soldier turned and abruptly left the room before Adam could take a shot.

"Shit!" he growled under his breath. Then he set off after the agent, moving cautiously past the pile of dead and smelly aliens.

The Unidor agent went through a series of doorways and into a much larger chamber where another guard stood watch over a group of Ladhi workers, all dressed in white kitchen uniforms. The guard began counting, waving his hand.

"All right, the next eight. Move up."

Adam was shocked to see that the workers anxiously obeyed, seeming almost excited that their turn had come. Something wasn't right. He scanned the faces, confirming that they were okay with what was about to happened to them.

Then he saw a face he recognized.

It was Idera. She was in the next group of eight moving up. She had on a Ladhi uniform and was one of the few faces that didn't look happy. Relieved, but not happy.

Adam laid back. He knew where they would be taken, and that only one of the guards would be with them. He rushed back the way he'd just come, finding a place to hide where he could come up behind the agent without being seen.

A few seconds later, the eight workers moved past him with the guard on their six. That was when Adam jumped out, performing the same choke-and-snap maneuver he'd done in the landing bay.

He had to shush the Ladhi quiet; they were genuinely upset.

"Adam?" Idera said in a loud whisper. "What are you doing here? And why did you kill him?"

"Why? Are you crazy?"

"He was taking us to a shuttle; they are letting us go."

"Letting you go?" Adam looked at the sea of angry faces. "Follow me."

Adam took Idera and pulled her around the corner. She nearly vomited when seeing the pile of dead workers. Several of the Ladhi who followed did vomit, only adding to the foul odor.

"They were taking you away in small groups so the rest of you wouldn't panic and start a riot."

"I did not know. Now, I must thank you for saving my life."

The Ladhi had the same idea. Adam waved them away. He reached down and took the MK from the dead guard. He handed it to Idera.

"How many guards are there?" he asked her.

"Just the one is left. Let us take him out."

"My thoughts exactly." Idera's beautiful golden eyes literally glowed. Adam hadn't noticed how beautiful they were until now.

Imploring the Ladhi to stay back and let the two mercenaries handle it, Adam and Idera returned to the staging area. They weren't subtle about it, blasting the unsuspecting guard with a pair of accurate bolts before he knew what was happening ... and much to the horror of the waiting Ladhi. There were about fifty of them, and Adam nearly had a riot on his hands until a few of the other workers came out and told them what had happened to their friends and co-workers. Some cried, but most simply collapsed out of disappointment. They thought they were being freed. Not anymore.

"I can take them to the lifeboats," Idera announced anxiously, stepping forward and waving her hand toward one of the large exit doors.

"No, you can't," Adam said. "They're all locked down. There's no way off the Station, not for a group this big."

"Then what are we to do?" asked one of the female service workers.

"You need to stay here. Lock yourselves in a storage locker until given the all-clear. Take plenty of food and water in with you. There's no telling how long this will take."

They understood, and a few of the senior workers took control, leading the group into other rooms where they began to gather food and water. They knew the kitchen area; they knew where they could hide.

Adam turned to Idera. "What are you doing here?"

"Following my intuition. When you did not leave the Station, I figured I would stay, as well. I wanted to see behind the scenes, to learn what was really happening. I figured what better way to remain unseen than to join the service staff."

Adam could tell she wanted to ask why he was shirtless and covered with tiny red dots, but she knew that could wait until later. Instead, she asked the all-important question.

"What are we to do now?" Idera asked.

Adam leaned against a wall. He was weary to his bones and weak from hunger. "Let's see, I—we—have killed eight of the terrorists total, out of maybe twenty-four. That leaves fifteen—"

"Sixteen."

"What?"

"There are sixteen left."

"What did I say?"

"Fifteen."

Adam shook his head. He was on the verge of passing out, and his brain was fuzzy, as was his math.

"You're right. There are sixteen left."

"We could try for the landing bay," Idera said. "But I assume that is locked down as well. Do you think our companions will be coming soon? I have been waiting."

Adam shook his head. "It will be a long wait."

He gave her the *Cliff Notes* of what happened to the MOB-4 and the fleet. When he was done, he watched Idera's bronze face turn to stone.

"Then we must kill the rest of them. Since you are not good with numbers, that is eight for each of us."

Adam grinned. "A piece of cake. I kill eight aliens before breakfast each morning."

Her expression went blank. "You do?"

He waved his hand. "Not really; it's a Human expression."

She stared at him for a few seconds. "About killing aliens? You do realize, that to you, *I* am an alien, as you are to me? You Humans are an odd species."

"No argument there." Adam looked around the room. It was now vacant except for him, Idera and the dead Unidor agent. "But first things first; I really need something to eat. Seeing that you're dressed like a food service worker, where can a guy get a meal around here? I can't kill aliens on an empty stomach."

"We found them in the food preparation section, one killed physically, the other by multiple flash bolts." Ror Hazz was literally frothing at the mouth from anger. He had a small cloth with him which he used to wipe away the spittle.

"It is The Human; he is back," stated Sandon Amick.

He and Ror were in one of the master suites on Level A where the Big Five were being kept. Amick had a datapad with him, charting the receipt of ransom payments being received. He insisted that there be five individual payments, one for each of the Elites. Three had been received, while the other two were still gathering the funds, not from their coffers, but from the planets with surviving minor Delegates. Even though both the Tel'orans and the Velosians could supply the full ransom and not even notice it on their ledgers, they told Kimm Vors that they were waiting for more contributions to come from others. Even the poorer worlds were contributing whatever they could. Amick laughed when told that the lowly Lep'sorians had donated five million credits to the cause, which to them was like a billion compared to the economies of others. That was ironic.

Amick tried to mirror the anger he saw in Ror about the deaths of their fellow mercenaries, but he couldn't, not fully. Eight had been killed, which meant larger shares for the rest of them. In the most pragmatic way, Amick would prefer The Human to kill all the others except him. But that wasn't practical or safe. Of course, he couldn't express that to Ror.

"Put together two teams of four and send them out into the Station. Maintain constant communications. We must hunt down The Human and quickly. The ransom will be paid soon, and then we will move to the landing bay, taking our special guests with us." He grinned. "They have yet to serve their full potential."

Ror rushed off to assign the teams.

Amick leaned back in the chair in the security office. He had to admit this alien—the Human—was a most-efficient killer, something Amick had to respect. He was pretty accomplished himself. Of course, he'd heard of the Humans for years, even worked with a few on a more cordial basis. But this one seemed especially skilled—and determined. Amick laughed. *I did not leave him much option*, he thought. Kill or be killed does not leave much room for compromise. But knowing that he was back aboard Rizen Station gave Amick a target and one he would not underestimate again. And eventually, The Human's luck would run out. Hopefully, it would occur before Amick ran out of agents.

Chapter 21

Idera led Adam to a bank of standard food processors that were able to spit out any number of individual meals, and once his blood was sampled, Adam chose three items from the menu. Seconds later, he was scarfing down a ham sandwich—a passable version—while stuffing processed chocolate chip cookies and beef jerky into his pockets. He would eat them on the way. They couldn't stick around the galley for long. The agents would be expected to check in periodically, and when they didn't, others would be sent to investigate.

The pair entered the C Concourse and hurried along for a couple of hundred feet before entering one of the side service corridors with the master keycard he still had. Adam wanted to say he knew where he was, but that wasn't the case. All the corridors looked the same. This was just one of the hundreds just like it. But he was more familiar with the internal elevator system. They found a car and entered.

"We can't kill the bad guys unless we know where they are," Adam told Idera. "And waiting for them to find us is a bad idea. We have to take the fight to them."

"Agreed," said his enthusiastic partner. "I understand the Delegates met in rooms above Level A, at the top of the Station. That was where they were taken hostage. They would not have been moved far."

Adam nodded. "Sounds right. And from what I saw in the broadcast, the main hostages, the Elites, were separated from the others. That would make two groups that have to be guarded. Figure at least two agents each, and the sixteen remaining is down to twelve who are mobile. It's a good bet some of them will be in roving teams out looking for us. And there would have to be more than one team. I took out a team of three in the landing bay, so assume the teams are larger than that; four-person teams at the minimum. Eight soldiers wandering the corridors leave only four to run things. They will be the leaders, including that Amick character. We take them out, and the unit will be headless."

"Where would they be?"

"The security office," Adam announced. "Unidor would have moved in when the regular Station force left. It would have comm and video and probably even an armory."

"And where is the security office?"

"I have no idea, but there has to be a directory somewhere aboard this floating unicycle."

Idera let the indecipherable word *unicycle* slide by. She was used to Adam punctuating his sentences with offbeat references. Descriptive, but lost on the alien.

"Perhaps this will help." She pointed at a mesh screen in the elevator's wall, like a speaker's cover.

"Voice activated?" Adam asked. Until now, the elevator doors operated by sensors with the cabs stopping at every floor. Could it be they did that because they had no other input? Adam would feel sick if that was the case, and he didn't know better.

He stepped up to the screen. "Security office," Adam spoke clearly into the speaker, hoping that if it were a voice-guided AI, it would have a translation feature.

It turned out that it did. But what it didn't have was common sense. Adam was looking for the security office and not reporting a security breach, which is what the computer thought he was doing.

Lights began to flash in the cab and the car bounced to a stop. An electronic voice came out of the speaker, instantly converted into English by his translation bug.

"State your emergency. Officers have been summoned. If the alert was in error, recite the cancel code now."

This was a Ladhi service elevator, used mainly by staff aboard the Station. They would have been briefed on security protocols, including the various codes needed to move about the Station. Neither Adam nor Idera had the codes. So the alarm kept blaring.

If the terrorists had taken over the security office, they would surely have been alerted to the commotion taking place in one of the hundreds of service elevators. Adam looked around and quickly spotted the camera lens. He took out his MK and blasted it.

Idera wasn't expecting it and began screaming at him for lighting off a flash bolt in such a confined area. She calmed down when she saw he'd shot out the camera.

Adam tried the emergency open button, assuming it was the emergency open button. None of the buttons worked. The elevator was stationary, and the door was locked. Nothing like offering themselves up to the terrorists on a silver platter.

He looked at the ceiling, seeing standard-issue segmented panels and lighting strips. One of the panels had to be an emergency access hatch. All elevators had them, didn't they?

"Idera, climb on my shoulders and test the panels for a way out."

She looked at him. "Can you support me?"

Adam smirked. "Pretty sure. C'mon, hurry."

She did as he asked. As a thin-boned alien, Adam had no trouble holding her up, and she easily reached the ceiling, probing each panel until one opened outward.

"I have found it!"

"Good, climb up. I'll follow."

The opening was narrow but made for Ladhi, which were aliens of average size—for aliens. Idera fit through easily. Adam was preparing to jump when the elevator door suddenly slid open. There were four aliens dressed in Unidor uniforms staring at him with thirsty looks on their varied faces, each with Xan-fis aimed at him. Adam glanced up to see the hatch in the ceiling slowly and silently close. He held his arms away from his body and grinned—a toothless, friendly grin.

"We have captured The Human," said one of the agents without pressing a comm device. They had to be on an open link.

"Is he completely subdued?" asked a voice Adam recognized from the broadcast as that of Sandon Amick.

"Momentarily."

Two of the agents rushed into the car and disarmed him. They patted his pants, not bothering to search his bare chest and back for additional weapons. They nodded to the leader.

"Subdued and disarmed."

"Very good," said Amick. "Use extreme caution—I repeat—extreme caution. I wish to meet this troublesome alien. Bring him to the security department. Can he hear me?"

"Yes."

"Then he will hear when I tell you to set your weapons on Level-1, and you have my permission to shoot at the slightest provocation. Meeting him is more of a curiosity than a necessity. Is that understood?"

"Yes, Amick."

"Does The Human understand?"

Adam nodded.

"He does."

"Good. Now bring him to me."

Unsurprisingly, all four of the agents entered the elevator with Adam. He felt the barrels of three Xan-fis pressing against the bare flesh of his back as he was pressed against the back wall and held there. The fourth agent went to the speaker and spoke "2234," and the car began to move.

Adam glanced up at the ceiling, wondering how Idera was fairing. He knew that most alien elevator systems ran by magnetics along the walls and not by cables as on Earth. The cars could move vertically and horizontally, so there was a good bet Idera was safe atop the car.

****

It was a fairly long journey to the Rizen Station security department, but they made it in a single elevator car after several upward and lateral movements. When the door opened, the guards hurried out and held weapons on Adam, motioning for him to exit. As he did, he glanced down. On the floor was a growing pool of blood about three inches in diameter. Before he left the cab, another drop fell past his vision. It—and the pool—were unseen by the guards. He cast his eyes up, seeing a line of red outlining the ceiling panel with the hidden hatchway.

Adam's assumptions had been wrong. Idera had anything but a leisurely ride atop the cab.

Adam's day was about to get a whole lot worse.

Chapter 22

Adam was led down a carpeted hallway that wasn't typical of the other service corridors. This one was a step up but still not as opulent as the main guest Concourses. In his travels within the Station, he'd seen several sections like this; they were the nervous system of the Station, including command and control, environment, guest services and other important functions. Security would also be a major department at a facility this large and one catering to a civilian clientele with lots of credits. Keeping them safe would be priority number one.

When he finally reached the department, Adam was mildly disappointed. Like the backlot at Disneyland, this was a utilitarian cluster of offices and monitoring stations located next to an equally basic sick bay. The rooms were empty except for the four guards escorting him and one tall, slender alien with an angular face, a goatee and slight grey skin. His eyes were dark with thick, caterpillar-like eyebrows below a full head of wavy black hair. Seeing that the alien terrorist leader was playing the part of Alan Rickman in *Die Hard*, Adam looked for any similarities. There weren't many; maybe the grey skin blew the illusion. But if there was one thing the two villains had in common, it was their manner of speaking.

"What an honor it is to finally meet the incomparable Human," Amick began. He was seated behind a plain work desk in a modest-sized office, wearing an impeccably tailored version of the Unisor uniform. He wore it well. But unlike Hans Gruber in his John Phillips suit, the alien's uniform revealed long ripples of muscle under the fabric and an overwhelming sense of animal strength. Where Gruber was a dandy, Amick was a danger.

"As a fellow traveler among the mercenaries of the galaxy, I must admit to a tinge of hero worship. I have had many contacts with Humans throughout the years—I even worked with a pair on

Rassenmore. They were incredible beings of extraordinary ability, as are you. The reputation of the one they call *The Human* precedes you."

Adam had trouble believing the translation he was hearing. Not the words but the tone. He knew the Formilian language database took English words and then searched synonyms for the best native equivalent based on some mysterious algorithm. It made all aliens sound more charming and articulate than they probably were in their native tongue. Adam was sure he sounded the same to them. Still, he found Sandon Amick to be an interesting and challenging adversary, although, at the moment, *adversary* was the wrong word. That assumed an equivalency that didn't exist. *Executioner* was a better fit.

"Please wait outside," Amick said to the guards. "I do not fear The Human. I can see in his manner that he has accepted his fate."

"I wouldn't assume so much."

Amick grinned. "Now, there is one thing that has intrigued me for years: What is your actual name?"

"Roy, Roy Rogers. Yippie-ki-ay, mother—"

"I do not believe you; you volunteered the name too easily." He waved his hand impatiently. "It matters not. I would not believe anything you tell me, although I do not know why you would lie. You have not many minutes left in your life to waste them on falsehoods."

"Then why don't you blast me with the MK? Let's get this over with; I've never liked the smell of alien. Killing me would put me out of my misery."

"Ah, but then it would rob me of the opportunity to practice my art."

"The art of killing?"

"Precisely!" Amick bounced in the chair. "You will see presently what I mean. It is an art form I myself have perfected. You will be quite impressed ... for a short while. After that, you will be part of it."

"I can hardly wait."

The door opened, and another alien bounded in. He had also been in the broadcast, placing a bolt into the back of the Unidor executive's head while Amick put one in Enrick Vor. He saw Adam and went for his MK.

"What is *he* doing here? Why have you not killed him?"

"Calm yourself, Ror—"

Adam laughed. "Roar? Your name is Roar? You must have been a naughty child."

"I was *not* a child!"

"Then that explains it."

"He is dangerous," Ror continued. "Have you forgotten the fallen members of our team?"

"Of course not. But consider how many extra credits The Human has made us."

"With fewer to share in the ransom?"

"Precisely."

"That is a sorry consolation," said Ror. "Most had been with us for years. And this beast killed them."

"As they would surely have done to him. You and I live in a world where the fastest MK is the victor. And before you sits the paragon of our profession ... *The Human*."

"Stop playing your games with him. Kill him so we can leave."

"The ransom?"

"It is all here. The accounts are full."

"Most excellent." Amick looked at Adam and smiled, a full, toothy smile. "I love it—"

"When a plan comes together?"

"Precisely!"

"Dude, you've been watching too many movies."

Amick frowned. "What is a *movie*?" The translation was slow. "Oh, a recording, a broadcast often for entertainment purposes. Yes, I have watched many, but sadly, none from Earth."

"That's too bad. Because if you had, you would know what's coming next."

"And what might that be?"

"Just that the hero always wins. And in this story, I'm the hero."

Amick slapped the desktop with his free hand. "See, Ror, what a delight it is to speak with a Human." He looked at Adam. "I have told him such many times before. Everything your species says sounds like … like a movie!"

"Amick!"

The terrorist leader waved his hand. "Yes, I know. I am just having a little fun before we go." Amick stood up and handed Ror a key card. "Get the Elites and take them to the ships. I will unlock the Bay doors. Wait for us. We will be along shortly."

"We? Are *we* going somewhere?" Adam asked.

"The *we* I refer to sadly does not include you."

"Why are you taking the Elites?" Adam followed up. "You have your credits. I thought you would set them free."

"I may very well do such a thing, just not now."

"Why not?"

Amick snorted. "For many reasons, of which the primary is we must escape. With them aboard our ships, no military vessel will dare fire upon us. I am sure there are already Ladhi warships just outside sensor range waiting for us to leave. Also, they may still produce revenue. Our Cartel and Pirate friends may appreciate the opportunity to speak with them, to do their own negotiations for their lives … for a fee. Besides, we have already agreed to assist the Cartels, but that assistance is at no charge."

"So, you are working for the Cartels."

Amick shook his head. "That we are not. Although, when this plan was devised, we did contact them, asking that they not interfere. They agreed but asked a favor in return."

"What favor?"

"That we destroy Rizen Station on our way out. They were quite serious about disrupting the conference. By offering to blow up the facility for free, they could not refuse."

Adam grimaced. "You see, this facility has a substantial monetary value. I cannot allow you to destroy it. You don't have that authority. You're just a grunt."

For all his admiration of Human-speak, Amick was at a loss. Part of the phrase translated, but others didn't, like the accurate translation of the word *grunt*.

"I take it you're not a fan of the *Alien* movies," Adam said, seeing the confusion on Amick's face. "I don't know why not. After all, you're an alien."

Amick looked to Ror. "Go, gather the Elites. I am beginning to weary of The Human's word games. We will be along shortly."

Ror didn't have to be told twice. He was out the door a second later.

"Come, Mr. Human. Time for an art lesson." Amick waved his MK at Adam. The four guards outside had been watching through the glass walls. Now they readied for escort duty.

"We are going to the Observation Pod. As you know, this beast is dangerous. Stay back and cover."

Adam snapped his teeth at the guards. "Yes, Iceman, I am dangerous."

Hey, with only minutes to live, Adam might as well have fun with the time he had left.

Chapter 23

The Observation Dome sat atop the Station above Level A. Since the gravity from the internal generators was exponential in effect, Level A had a little less gravity that Level B, and so forth. That left the Observation Dome with gravity equivalent to about a third that of Earth, or about the same as Mars.

Adam and his five-alien-escort was led into the huge chamber, lit by the constant brilliance of the planet Rizen. It was an impressive room about half the size of a circular football field with glass walls extending to the floor. It truly did seem as if you were standing on the surface of the Station and with the vastness of space all around you. The only thing breaking the effect were the seven thick modules spaced regularly along the circumference.

"These are airlocks," Amick started the narration, "which allow guests to don spacesuits, and while on tethers, to walk the surface of the Station. The more adventuresome may use jet packs to journey beyond it for a time in free flight. Since there is gravity even outside the Dome, most opt to simply walk along the hull." Amick stepped up to the thick glass dome and placed a hand on it. "During the investigation phase of the operation, I spent some time at Rizen Station as a tourist. I even afforded myself a walk along the hull. It is quite stimulating."

"Yeah, I know," Adam said, recalling his brief escapade outside the kitchen area.

"Now, let me explain what is about to happen."

The guards stood around Adam at a safe distance, their weapons pointed at him.

"I am fascinated with the *moment* of death, when the spirit realizes that this is the end, that all memory and sensation is to be no more. Because of this, I discovered a new artform I call Frozen Death. To achieve this, I have my subjects exposed to the harsh cold of space, flash freezing them at that moment between life and death. In their faces and in their body configurations, I have found the ultimate expression of true art. It is art of life and of death, captured at such a moment because I control the timing. It is quite beautiful."

"So says the psychopath."

Amick worked through the translation. "That is correct. I revere death, I do not fear it or find it distressing."

"You should try it sometime. It's not all it's cracked up to be."

Amick frowned. The words were right, but the meaning cryptic. He let it go.

"In a few moments, you will enter the chamber, but without a spacesuit. I will then let in the absolute cold of space. Following, I will pressurize the chamber to expel your frozen body. The gravity will take affect and you will drift back down onto the Dome. There I will relish and record my latest masterpiece. Unfortunately, I will not have time to fully savor the moment; I have other issues to tend to. But be assured, I will cherish this moment even greater than most. As I have mentioned, I have much respect for your heroism and accomplishments."

"So much so that you're going to freeze me. That doesn't make sense."

"Of course, it doesn't. This is *death* we are talking about. It is what living beings avoid the most. But just think, in a few moments, you will have no more worries, no more needs or wants. You will truly be free."

"Yeah, until someone brings you back to life," Adam whispered under his breath.

"I did not hear that."

"Never mind. It's not important." Adam looked at the guards. "You know, I could spoil the moment by rushing your agents and have them shoot me dead in a more conventional fashion. That would ruin your masterpiece." Adam spun his finger into the air as he said *masterpiece*, emphasizing the word. "I'm not about to voluntarily walk into—"

The first flash bolt took out the agent directly in front of Adam. It was a strong Level-2 and on target. In the dim light of the Dome, the bolt was blinding, but Adam's Human reactions were already about to pounce rather than be forced into the airlock. He just let the moment carry him, moving in light gravity and not questioning where the bolt had come from. It didn't matter. He was at the next guard a split second later, with a left to the chin followed by a right uppercut.

There were more flash bolts going off, both from the terrorists and the unknown shooter. Unknown? Adam knew who it was: Idera. She wasn't as injured as he first thought.

She was at the entrance to the Dome, a stairway that led up out of the floor. She was hunkered down for cover and firing at the three surviving terrorists, including Amick. He and two of his agents were inside the reenforced airlocks, the only cover in the room.

Adam scooped up a Xan-fi and turned just in time to see one of the agents get a bead on him. He dived for the deck, pulling a dead agent on top of him. The body took the brunt of the bolt.

Since that worked, Adam lifted the body in the light gravity and used it as a shield as he ran for the hole in the floor. Bolts were either zipping by his head, splashing on the deck or hitting the dead guard. Either way, the temperature in the Dome was climbing from the proliferation of star-hot plasma bolts.

Adam fell headfirst into the stairwell as Idera kept up a steady barrage of covering fire. She paused only for a couple of seconds as she snapped another battery pack into the MK. Adam bounced on the stairs, saved only by the one-third gravity in the stairwell.

He was up in a second tugging at Idera. "Let's go!"

"No! We can kill the leader. He is trapped."

"We can't kill him. We have to let him live."

Idera glanced down at him as if he were crazy before going back to firing.

"There's a bomb on board the Station," he yelled up at her. "If we kill him, there's no reason for the others to stay, and they'll set off the bomb. They won't set it off as long as he's still on board. We have to get to the landing bay. They've taken the Elites there."

She understood, and after saturating the Dome room with three quick bolts, she ducked down and jumped to the landing below the stairs. There was a pressure door leading to the stairs and the Dome. Adam slammed it behind her and then placed a bolt in the electronic control pad. Sparks flew and the door was locked.

Adam stepped back, taking in the alien female mercenary. She had blood all over her, but with a piece of Unidor uniform wrapped around her left thigh. She saw Adam focus on the bandage.

"I would not recommend riding on the outside of an elevator car. And about the bandage? One of the terrorists volunteered his uniform, at the expense of his life."

Adam grinned while refreshing his calculations. Counting the agent Idera killed earlier, plus the two in the Observation Dome, they were up to eleven dead, leaving thirteen still in the Station. There was a good chance everyone but the three in the Dome would be in the Landing Bay, waiting for Amick. Ten soldiers of fortune ... waiting.

"Are you able to move?" Adam asked Idera.

"I moved here, did I not? I am fine. And here, this might help." She handed him a datapad. "It contains destination codes for the elevators. We can get to the landing bay directly from anywhere."

"Then let's go. I don't know how crazy these guys are. They may blow the Station just out of spite."

"Explain *blow the Station*?"

"Blow it up, like set off the bomb."

"Yes, *that* we must prevent. There should be no blowing. Let us go."

There was an elevator near the entrance to the Observation Dome since the venue was a major attraction aboard the Station. Adam scanned the datapad, which in one configuration showed the destination codes by map and not by name. He spoke the code, and the cab shot off.

Chapter 24

Idera wasn't in as good a shape as she let on. She leaned against the side of the elevator car, looking as if she was about to pass out.

"I thought you were dead," Adam said tenderly.

"So did I. But somehow, I held on. The car moves incredibly fast and makes erratic turns."

Adam smiled. "Oh, and thanks for saving my life. I was about to become Amick's last masterpiece."

"Masterpiece?"

"As in artwork. He's really into dead bodies."

"In what manner?" She looked thoroughly disgusted.

"Never mind; I was making a joke. But seriously, thanks for saving me."

"I owed you from before. Now we are zero."

Adam took that as meaning they were even.

"There could be as many as ten agents at the end of this ride," he said, refocusing the pair of Indie mercenaries.

"I am glad your math is better. I already had that worked out."

"How many packs do you have? I only have what's left in this Xan-fi." He checked it. "Half a charge."

"I took three packs from the agent I killed to get the bandage and datapad." She grinned, knowing the sarcasm in her statement. Unfortunately, her battery packs were for MKs and not Xan-fis. The two rival weapon makers had never made compatible packs, choosing to keep them proprietary. That left Adam in the lurch until he could grab packs from a dead alien. He was sure there would be more than enough in the landing bay. Dead aliens that is, at least after he and Idera got through with them

But it still meant that Idera would have to carry the load, at least initially. Even though she had proven her worth in both the kitchen and the Observation Dome, Adam was almost tempted to ask to trade weapons with her. After all, he was the great Human warrior, a legend across the galaxy. But then he hesitated. Since he did have more natural abilities than she did, Idera would need the weapon and battery packs more than he. Also, she could be killed by Level-2 bolts; he couldn't. He concluded he would use the gifts given to him from Mother Nature to carry his weight in the coming fight.

****

The problem with riding in an ultra-quiet and smooth-running elevator car was one didn't know when the damn thing would suddenly slide to a stop and open the doors. The other thing, they didn't know where in the landing bay they would end up. Both mercs panicked when the car stopped unexpectedly, and the doors opened. They lifted their guns, ready to shoot anything outside the elevator.

They didn't have to. They were in the wide and gaudy commercial district outside the landing bay, and as before, it was deserted. It was also about a quarter mile from the main bays. Adam had to help Idera get moving; her leg had stiffened.

Adam knew where the Unidor starships were located—in Bay 3. The seven bays weren't lined up according to which came first for the tourists. Instead, the main concourse began at Bay 4, with three bays to the left and three to the right, reducing the walking time for guests departing the shuttles. The fact that Adam and Idera dumped out of the elevator early helped their cause. It gave them time to sneak up on Bay 3, listening for sounds and alert to the green and black uniforms of the enemy.

At the main airlock to Bay 3, they could see that it was open and hushed voices emanated from inside. They sounded stern and serious, with orders being cast in professional tones. Amick must have communicated with his second-in-command, the alien named Roar. Adam was pretty sure it wasn't spelled *r-o-a-r*, but it didn't matter. That's what it sounded like. Roar was setting the defensive perimeter, anticipating the arrival of Adam and his unknown accomplice. In addition, there may be a pair of guards rushing off to free Amick and the other two agents from the Observation Dome. Adam hadn't thought that one through all the way, but it did buy them time to get to the landing bay.

Each bay consisted of a set of massive airlocks. Incoming starships would enter the wide access port and then move to the assigned bay. The compartment would be stripped of its air and the outer door would slide open. Once inside, the atmosphere would return and then the inner door would open.

Adam and Idera crouched near the inner door, hiding behind a kiosk that sold processed food bars of a sweet nature. It was on wheels, so they slowly moved it across the concourse so they could get a better look into the bay.

Adam had been in there about five to six hours ago. He semi-knew the layout. There were ample defensive locations and excellent cover, able to provide crossfire from multiple locations. It wouldn't be easy to get in the bay without being seen and even harder to penetrate deeper with just two of them moving from point to point on the deck. That was what made Adam look up.

Although the bay was a sealed unit, it had an open ceiling, just like the concourse. Black painted piping, electrical conduits and other equipment covered the ceiling, partially disguised by the color of the paint and the height of about one hundred feet. At the bulkhead to the bay, massive pressure doors would slide over and seal the compartment. Then at the boundary between the concourse and the airlock, the equipment fed through the bulkhead and came out the other side.

Adam pointed up. "I think we can slip over the door threshold from up there and then get the drop on the bad guys from the high ground."

Idera smiled. "I see the strategy, even though I am lost in your description. But not both of us. Once the enemy is focused on the high shooter, the other should be able to slip in on ground level."

"That works, too. I'll go high."

"No, let me."

"But your leg."

"I will not use my legs." She held out a long, slender arm. "My people are known for our climbing abilities. The strongest part of our bodies are the arms. I can easily scale the wall and move along the overhead without using my legs, at least not to a full degree."

"Don't forget the range of the MK." It was only about a hundred feet with any accuracy.

"Gravity will assist. I will be shooting down."

Adam nodded. It sounded like a good plan. And it might give him a chance to get inside and take out at least one agent so he could get his weapon and power packs. At the moment, Adam was feeling vulnerable with only ten shots left at Level-2.

"Do you see a path up?"

Idera smiled again. "I will create my own path. Trust me; this is exciting for me. I need this to restimulate my system. For a while, I was letting my leg govern my mood. I am ready for some action."

Damn, I like her! Adam thought. *She's an alien after my own heart.*

"Okay, just make sure you have good cover before you open fire. You can probably get up there without being seen because no one will be looking up. But once the shooting starts, they'll know instantly where you are."

"I will target the agent closest to you by the door, giving you an access point."

"Let's do it. I have a feeling Amick and the others might be on their way here by now. Let's hit them before they can get any reinforcements."

****

They pushed the cart back until their movements were blocked by the airlock door then rushed across the concourse at the boundary between Bay 3 and Bay 4. There were plenty of handholds here for Idera to begin her climb. And climb she did. Resembling a spider monkey from Earth, she used one spindly arm to lift her to the next handhold rocking back and forth, moving with incredible speed and confidence; in fact, Adam was shocked at the fluidity of her movements, like the greatest Olympic gymnast on the uneven parallel bars. It was as if she could tell instinctively where to go next. She didn't miss a beat and never had to backtrack.

Adam grinned proudly, as if Idera was his protégé and she was performing beyond expectations. Then he thought: Just as his species had special traits that set them apart from others, every race had *something* that made them special. It may not apply in the realm of special operations, but there was something, even if they could stack cups faster than anyone else in the galaxy. It was the first thing that came to his mind.

Idera reached the ceiling and waved at him, smiling. *Show-off,* he thought. And then she was gone a moment later, making the transition from the concourse to inside the bay with insane ease.

She was out of sight now, so Adam moved closer to the open portal. Any agents guarding the doorway would have their eyes glued on the lower portion and at either side of the opening; he dare not do a look-see. Adam and Idera had already surveyed as much of the interior as they could see from the kiosk. It wasn't much, and all they caught were glimpses of the agents as they moved into position. He would have to go in blind, relying on his Human reactions to make decisions on the fly. His guide would be the location of Idera's first shots. Once she started raining fire down on the Unidor soldiers from above, they would have to look up. That is when he would enter.

Unfortunately, they didn't have comm devices. Adam would have to go at the first burst of plasma light.

A full minute went by, making Adam suspect Idera was having trouble finding cover in the overhead. *That's fine; take your time. Let's do this right.*

Then came the flash, followed a fraction of a second later by the poof of the bolt launcher. Adam was around the doorway a heartbeat later, sighting where the first bolt had hit. It was only about twenty feet away, and with his Human speed, he was there another heartbeat later. He dove over a row of chemical barrels and landed heavily on the smoking body of a Unidor soldier. He made it without any bolts coming his way, but that changed almost immediately. Just from the sound of the weapons, he estimated there were three guards remaining at the entrance. Two were firing at him, while the other aimed high.

Adam scooped up the agent's Xan-fi and then rifled through his utility belt for more battery packs. He replaced the cartridge in his current rifle and then shouldered it. He would take both weapons with him, plus the agent's MK. One could never have too much firepower.

He was up a moment later returning fire with Human accuracy. He looked up and pinpointed Idera's location. It wasn't hard to find. She was ensconced between a pair of huge rail tractors, fairly well hidden and popping off MK bolts every couple of seconds. Adam used the false beam nature of the brilliant bolts to locate his targets. He took out one guard and then another before the last one cut tail and ran farther into the Bay, disappearing around the bulk of shuttlecraft.

Ten agents—at the most—minus three. Only seven of the bastards left. Until Amick and the two he had with him arrived. Adam had to hurry.

Once the shooting stopped, Adam looked up to see Idera swing from her hiding place and make her way to the inner bulkhead with the pressure door into the Station. She was back on the deck and meeting up with him in less than thirty seconds.

"Impressive," Adam said.

"I thought you would like that," Idera blushed. "Where to next?"

Adam motioned with his hand. "There are four Unidor ships located off to the right and at the back of the Bay, near the outer pressure door. Amick mentioned he would unlock the doors. We have to be careful that they don't climb in their ships and then close the inner door. They'll be able to flush us out, along with the atmosphere in the chamber."

"What about Amick?"

"They can repressurize once we're taken care of."

"Then let us hurry. They are on the run. Let us keep them off balance."

****

After telling Idera he would take point, Adam rushed off for the Unidor ships, allowing her to follow on her bum leg. He darted between shuttles and other obstacles, coming up on the four sleek dark green and black-painted spacecraft only a few seconds later. The running guard barely beat him there.

Four other agents were outside the ships, including the one named Roar. They were in defensive positions and not inside the ships preparing to button them down. That was good. They hadn't thought to neutralize the threat by sucking the air out of the bay. Not yet.

Adam lit off a bolt while still in a full sprint at the fleeing agent, striking him cleanly in the back. Splash another bad guy. But then he had to take to the air, diving over more crates and barrels seeking cover from the barrage of incoming flash bolts. The Unidor soldiers were fair shots—for aliens—but it was the sheer number of bolts that overwhelmed Adam. He hunkered down until battery packs had to be changed out before jumping up and sprinting along the length of the first Unidor ship and sliding behind the cover of a line of storage containers most often towed by muleships. This changed the perspective of the shooters, turning them away from the direction Adam had come ... and from where Idera was about to appear.

The two mercs caught the Unidor troops in a crossfire, taking out two more. That would leave possibly four more, with two outside the ship and two inside if none had been sent to free Amick. The hostages had to be inside the ship.

Adam took a grazing hit from a plasma bolt on his right bicep, wincing in pain as the skin bubbled and stung. He could handle it; in fact, it only made him madder. He lifted up and sighted the shooter, delivering a killing bolt square on his long-snouted face.

They were down to three.

Ror cut for the hatchway into the ship. Bolts came out of the opening as more agents provided cover. Adam and Idera flooded the opening with bolts. They may not hit anything, but the heat, light and expanding nature of splashing bolts would be enough to distract them long enough for Adam to make it to the doorway.

With reckless abandon, an angry Adam Cain flew into the airlock, hitting Ror in the side and then tumbling over into another agent. The third one was lining up his Xan-fi on Adam's head.

Adam grabbed the barrel and shoved it away just as the agent triggered the weapon. It lit off, striking the alien below him in the neck. Next, Adam kicked out with his right leg, striking the soldier with the Xan-fi in the ribs. He fell over, piling on top of a still-disoriented Ror.

Adam didn't bother with the pair of Xan-fis and the one MK he had. Instead, he used brute strength, pummeling the two still living aliens with both his fists, hearing bone break and lungs collapse. He saved Ror for last. The Unidor officer's eyes were calm and aware as his body was racked with shock from his traumatic injuries. Adam noticed a glimmer of recognition—just what he was waiting for—before Adam placed the killing blow to the nose of the ugly alien, crushing the bone and ligament which penetrated the brain.

Adam pressed back from the pile of dead aliens and stared down at bodies. He smirked, again unable to restrain himself from making some total incomprehensible comment should anyone be listening.

"I am Human ... hear *me* Roar!"

Adam suddenly rolled over, pulling the MK and pointing it back toward the airlock entrance. He didn't fire. It was Idera. She had a frown on her face and was shaking her head.

"I suspect what you said has some meaning on Earth."

"It does.

"Not here."

Adam snorted.

A few minutes later, Adam and Idera were with the Elite hostages, all five of them. They kept them inside the ship in case Amick showed up. Adam had counted up the dead, concluding that all ten of the agents were in the bay. That left no one to free Amick. But still, he couldn't take the chance.

"We must leave now!" said the Tel'oran Salus Newish. His floppy green ears weren't so floppy at the moment, being stiffer and quivering slightly. "There was talk a bombs planted aboard the Station."

"Yeah, we know of that," Adam told him. "But no one's going to set them off with their leader still aboard."

"Sandon Amick still lives?" asked Polandin Davinor from Avion.

"We'll deal with him soon." Adam looked through the small sea of alien faces. "Where's Kimm, Kimm Jors?"

"The Lep'sorian?" Salus said wrinkling his large, flat nose. "We have not seen him in hours. He was not kept with us. Why ask, we must go."

"We're not going anywhere until we get the others, including Kimm,"

"Why? They are of no consequence."

"You're fellow Delegates? You don't care about them?"

"Of the fifteen, there are only nine left," said Polandin.

"And what about your staff? There are about fifty of them still alive."

"And what is your point?" Salus asked.

Adam recoiled. "You guys are a bunch of elitest assholes, aren't you?'

The translation—although guaranteed to be inaccurate—was nevertheless enough to let the aliens know they were being insulted.

"Enough of this banter!" Salus stated unequivocally. "I demand that you fly us away from here. The fate of others is none of our concern."

"Screw you!" Adam snapped back. "We aren't going anywhere until I say we are."

"You are the one they call The Human," said Polandin. "We have all had dealings with your kind. As crude as you are, you are equally obstinate. Consider all that has taken place to save the lives of the five of us. Should not that be an indicator as to who is more important here, a dwindling group of second-tier Delegates and their minions, or us? If you fail to answer correctly, then you are beyond reasoning."

"Then consider me beyond help."

Salus turned to Idera. "You are a Cos'minean. Your race has more common sense. You can fly us away."

Idera's leg was hurting and she was in no mood to play politics with the Elites. "I suggest you remain quiet, lest you become a casualty of this little war. I would hate for an MK to go off accidently in your direction."

Salus recoiled. "I shall remember your attitude, as well as that of The Human. You will be hearing from our respective governments."

Idera turned to Adam. "Do you think we would be held responsible should these five meet tragic ends during the course of this crisis?"

"Hey, we could always blame it on the terrorists." Adam stepped up to the taller, long-ear alien and placed a finger in his chest. "I suggest you do what she told you to do. We're in no mood for your bullshit."

The Elites looked at each, then Polandin asked, "What is the significance of bovine excrement in this conversation?"

Adam shook his head, giving up. Fortunately, a communicator on one of the dead Unidor agents became active.

"Adam Cain, can you hear me? It is Kimm Vors."

"You are Adam Cain!" Salus cried out. The other Elites gawked at him. "I should have known; yet I thought you would be much older."

Idera looked at Adam. "Is this a name I should know?"

"It's not important. Maybe I'll explain someday." He was rifling through the small stack of dead agents, looking for the communicator. He found it.

"Kimm, it's Adam. Where are you? How did you know I would have a Unidor communicator?"

"Oh, Adam. I am so glad to hear you are alive." The voice was the lower version of the tadpole's normal speaking voice, again the result of the metamorphosis he was going through. "I heard them speaking of how you took a communicator as this crisis was beginning. I found this one and took a chance. Can they hear me?"

"Maybe a few, but not many. There ain't that many of the terrorists left."

"That is welcome news. They took the Elites away recently. I fear for the fate of the rest of us."

"Are you with the other Delegates?"

"No, I am in my suite. I was injured. In the current state of my being, I believe it is serious. Can you help me?"

"Are you alone?"

"Yes. I am locked inside."

"What's your room number?" Adam couldn't find the suite earlier. He would need some guidance to find it this time.

Kimm gave it to him, along with directions and landmarks. Adam had the datapad with the map of the Station and the elevator codes. He found the nearest exit point.

But he hesitated. "Kimm, are you sure you're alone? I don't want this to be a trap; I'm in no mood. I'm going to come in ready to shoot. You better be clear if I see Amick or any of his other goons."

"I assume goons refer to his agents? I assure you I am alone. But please hurry. They have planted bombs on the Station. Once they leave, they will detonate the devices."

Adam smiled. "They aren't going anywhere." He didn't elaborate, knowing Amick was probably listening. And that was another problem. If Kimm truly was alone in his suite, he wouldn't be for long. Amick wasn't at the landing bay, so he was either still trapped in the Observation Dome or he was on his way to Kimm's suite. That's fine, Adam thought. Time to put this story to bed.

He turned to Idera. "Stay here and guard these assholes. There's a chance Amick may still show up. Lock the door. And remember, as long as Amick is onboard, he won't set off the bombs. I'll get Kimm, and the others, too, if I can. The four Unidor ships can get them all out, including the staff. I think the only chance we have is to get off the Station before Amick does."

"What about the service workers in the kitchen?"

"Sorry, sweetheart, but we can't save everyone."

"That is unfortunate. Go now, and hurry back. I will keep these five from doing anything stupid. I only hope I can restrain myself." She glared at Salus and Polandin. They got the message.

Chapter 25

Adam was off a moment later. He still had to be careful not to run into Amick, which the more he thought of it, may be a non-issue. He should still be in the Observation Dome; there was no way out. If that were the case, Adam prayed he didn't have the detonator with him. Keeping him thinking he had options would prevent him from pressing the button. If he felt his situation was hopeless, he may decide to go out in a blaze of sick, demented glory, especially if he were aware his escape route had been cut off. But there were still a couple of dozen shuttles aboard, and he had their key.

Adam entered an elevator car and gave the code for a stop two stations past where Kimm said he could find the suite. He wasn't taking chances. He'd backtrack and pick off anyone watching the exit near the room.

He only came with an MK—a model 24—and three battery packs. They were easier to carry than the bulkier Xan-fi. Once he had Kimm, he'd have the Lep'sorian show him where the others were kept. It was true that the four Unidor ships could hold probably sixty people, and at the moment, all he was interested in was getting them off the station and to Ladhi. It may be crowded aboard the ships, but they didn't have far to go.

Even so, Amick was the wildcard. From Adam's experience, the more desperate the bad guys became, the more unpredictable. But Amick had five billion credits waiting in a bank account somewhere. That was a lot of incentive not to commit suicide.

Still, Adam was kicking himself for not being on one of the Unidor ships already and blasting away from the Station. That would have made the Elites happy, and Adam just might live a little longer. But instead, he was creeping up on Kimm's door, weapon in hand and not knowing what was waiting on the other side. But he felt a responsibility toward his client, especially someone he liked, although he didn't really care much about the others. He chuckled softly to himself as he neared the suite. Perhaps it was the hero in him that drove him forward. Or perhaps it was just that he didn't like to lose. Especially not to a smarmy bastard like Sandon Amick

His right shoulder hurt from the grazing hit he'd taken a few minutes ago, although most of the pin-prick wounds he'd suffered at the multiple hands of the centipede thing were nearly all gone. He was still shirtless, although he couldn't say why. He could have borrowed a garment from one of several dead Unidor soldiers. He just felt displaying his buffed torso would look better on the movie poster.

He shrugged off his exhaustion-induced silliness and approached the door, thinking how differently his day may have gone if he had found the suite the first time, rather than asking a Unidor soldier for directions. And then he shrugged again. If that were the case, he would have been on the MOB-4 when it blew up. Okay, here was better.

He still had the master key card and after listening through the door for any sounds, he quietly inserted it and waited for the answering click. He stood to one side and slowly pushed the door open.

Adam waited a few seconds before doing a look-see. The main living area anchored by the enormous picture window was empty, as far as he could tell. Recalling the layout from memory, he knew there was a bulbous vase in the small lobby on his side of the doorway. He slipped in, remaining low and slid in behind it. He heard a noise coming from the master bedroom area to the left.

"Kimm, is that you?"

"Oh, Adam! Wonderful, you made it."

"Are you alone?"

"I am. I am just finishing a meal."

Adam frowned. In the call, Kimm said he was injured and sounded much more in distress than he did now. And for that matter, here was the deeper voice from before. Perhaps this was how it would be from now until the transitioning.

"I'm coming to you," Adam announced.

He rushed forward, taking cover behind a long sofa arrangement. Against the wall behind him lay his duffle bag, filled with a variety of weapons he never got the chance to use. He knew Kimm was through the doorway next to the bag, but he kept his weapon focused on the entrance on the other side of the suite, where the staff had been invited to bunk down. All was quiet. Considering how few bad guys there were left on the Station, Kimm may very well be alone. If not, then Amick could also be in the room with Kimm, holding a gun to his rotund, bug-eyed head.

Adam went to the doorway and tried the handle. It was unlocked.

Adam burst through, slipping to his right and taking cover behind a table he remembered was there. And then he gasped, lifting his weapon, ready to shoot.

He was staring at the back of what could only be described as a man-size frog, but with differences. It was a Borr, complete with massive hind frog-like legs, smaller front limbs and a pair of normal looking arms and hands. The head was bulbous with the eyes set more in the skull than were those of the tadpoles—the Neos. But what set Adam off the most was the fact that the beast was delightfully munching away on the bloody carcass of Kimm Vors.

The limp and deflated body was half in the creature's mouth and half out of it, with inch-long white teeth gleefully tearing at the flesh. Adam stood and pointed the MK at the head of the beast.

"You disgusting, fucking freak."

The frog's head turned toward Adam, a set of deep creases in its expressive forehead. "You are referring to me? Why? Do you not consume the essence of your pupal stage? It is quite nourishing, with many essential vitamins and minerals my recently released body needs."

"You're Rion," Adam stated.

The frog rejoiced, opening his wide mouth and displaying his blood-coated teeth. "You remembered! Indeed, I am Rion."

"Aren't you a little premature? Kimm said you weren't due for a couple of weeks."

Adam relaxed somewhat, yet still disgusted by the bloody scene but accepting it as the way of the Lep'sorians. He went to the doorway and checked the living room again.

"I am indeed premature, but it was no accident."

"What do you mean?" Adam asked, more concerned with who might be in the staff wing of the suite than with the birthing habits of tadpoles and frogs.

"I was due to transition fully in ten days; we can time it almost to the hour. But that was until I fed Kimm a chemical the Borrs have developed that will speed up the process. It is quite experimental, but it worked."

Adam frowned. "You mean you intentionally—"

As Adam turned, he saw Rion holding an MK-17 in his very Human-like hand. "What the hell are you doing?"

"This..." Rion pulled the trigger, striking Adam in the bare chest with a stun bolt. The force of the blast pushed Adam into the living room and to the floor. The bolt wasn't as burning as a Level-1 or -2, but it did carry a higher electric charge. Adam spasmed slightly, allowing the MK to trickle from his hand. Awareness and coordination returned almost immediately and he went for the gun.

But by then, Amick and two of his goons emerged from the far room and pounced on him. Within a couple of seconds, Adam was back to his full Human self, but they already had restraints on his wrists and had thrown him onto the sofa. These were standard alien handcuffs and comparable to Human shackles on Earth. Adam knew how to snap them open using the connecting chain. All special operators knew how.

The two soldiers backed halfway across the room, well out of reach, with their guns focused on their prisoner. Amick was a little more daring. He stepped up to Adam and hit him with a powerful closed fist to the jaw.

Adam was beyond playing games. Unlike with the police officers on Anarea, he didn't pretend it hurt. Instead, he glared manic-eyed at Amick, watching as he rubbed his hurt hand. Human bones were like stone when compared to that of aliens.

"Please, sir, can I have some more?" Adam said in a childlike voice. Of course, the reference was lost on the alien.

Frustrated, Amick let out a quick laugh. "Why do I humor you? You must be surprised to see us here. You thought we were trapped in the Observation Dome. Did you not recall what I said about the airlocks? We simply donned spacesuits and walked to secondary access locks in the hull. We were free only minutes after you left us."

Adam shrugged. "Then why did you come here and not the landing bay? You could have been gone by now. Or you'd be dead—like the others."

Amick's face brighten, not the expression Adam was expecting.

"Then I thank you! Now there are ten less shares to give out. You, Adam Cain, are making me millions of credits with each team member you kill. I should put you on the payroll." He turned toward the door and yelled into Kimm's—Rion's—room. "Hurry, we must go."

"I am just finishing up," said Rion, and a couple of seconds later, he came through the door, having washed his face and hands of the remains of Adam's client. But was Rion also Adam's client? He dismissed the thought. He had more important things to think about.

"So, you're working for Amick now," Adam said acidly.

The frog/minotaur bellowed out a laugh. "Perhaps, Amick, it is time we inform our friend here as to the truth." On his four legs, Rion walked around to Adam's side of the couch. "This will come as a surprise to you, but I do not work for Amick; Amick works for *me*. Ah, I see the shock on your face. It is true. It was I who planned the operation and the takeover of Rizen Station."

It took a few moments for Adam to digest the revelation. At first, he was confused, but then it dawned on him. He became livid. "So,

Kimm knew about this all along. Great, you guys played me like a fiddle." If there was one thing Adam hated it was a traitor ... a traitor to him.

"Oh, Kimm did not know. He was a Neo, they have not a deceptive bone in their brittle bodies."

Now Adam was truly confused. "But how could you have done this? You were, what, a fetus growing on Kimm's back? And Kimm said you don't take over his brain. How do you know anything about anything? Hell, you were born just a few minutes ago."

"There is much you do not understand. It is true. I did not take all of Kimm's brain; however, the knowledge transfer was mainly one way, from him to me. During the transition stage, my mind becomes fully developed, and I am aware of all that goes on in the life of the Neo. Since the Neo is to die, there is no need for him to gain knowledge from me. This is the way we transition. It is quite natural. Also, at times before the transition, we can temporarily supplant the actions of the Neo with those of our own. The Neo is unaware of these episodes since they traditionally last only a few minutes to a few hours and are usually reserved for the final days before full transition. However, because of the drug I fed Kimm, I have had that ability for nearly two hundred days, and I have had it at will. It was during these sessions that I devised the plan, did the research and hired Amick and his team. It is also why I have been able to communicate with Amick during each stage of the operation, letting him know what you were doing. And now he and his remaining team will earn half a billion energy credits while I retain the rest."

"Kimm said the Borr aren't very intelligent ... but you sure are greedy."

Rion's eyes blinked wide. "You believe I did all this for the credits? No, my ambitions jump far beyond greed. I intend to use these credits to finance a revolution."

Adam smirked. "What revolution? On Lep'sor? That doesn't make sense."

"It makes perfect sense. Contrary to the Neo's impression of us, the Borr are highly intelligent and motivated. Unfortunately, we are also creatures of tradition. You must admit that the set-up of Lep'sorian society is counter to that of most others. This is because of tradition mostly. I intend to change all that by putting the Borrs in control of Lep'sorian society, making the weak and gentle Neos *our* servants. The change has been coming for generations. All we lacked were the resources. I have solved that problem."

"Wait, what? You're going to change how your people have done things for millions of years with a few billion credits? This is a joke, isn't it?"

"Why is it a joke? We have not gained more status in our society because we have been held back. The Borr are stronger, more mechanically capable and just as intelligent and innovative as the Neo. And all we need do is take control of the Neo facilities and place Borrs in charge."

"And just like that, things change overnight. Well, good luck with that."

"Come, Rion," Amick said impatiently. "The Human still has an accomplice, and we must find a way off the Station. They have my key card; we must use a shuttle."

Adam had to keep the Borr talking. The moment Rion stopped ... he was dead.

"Do you think the Sector is going to let you get away with this, allow you to go back to Lep'sor and play the great liberator? They'll be on you like flies on shit."

"Very descriptive," said Rion. "Having just emerged, I am quite stimulated by the new and creative. But, Adam Cain, you forget the Station is to be destroyed, at which time the Cartels will take credit.

They intend to rule the Sector through fear, and this act will certainly do that. I will bear no responsibility."

"And what, you just inherited more money than is in the global treasury of Lep'sor?"

"If you have not noticed, no one cares about Lep'sor. What we do on our planet will be of no concern to others." He waved his hand and then began to trot off toward the main door. One of the guards moved with him. "But now, I agree with Amick. It is time to close this chapter in my life and begin another. Amick, the detonator is on the table next to you. Bring it; we will now depart."

Adam's attention suddenly focused on the table and the small electronic box sitting atop it. Amick noticed, and he grinned. "Do not even contemplate, Adam Cain. You will not live to get the chance." The alien stepped forward and pointed his MK at Adam's chest. It wasn't set on stun. Adam tensed his legs, ready to jump...

****

One of Amick's troops had moved to open the outer door for Rion, and when he did, he took a Xan-fi blast directly to the chest. The brilliant flash temporarily blinded everyone in the room, Adam included. But although he couldn't see for a split second, he could still move. He pressed with his legs propelling himself over the back of the sofa, avoiding an MK bolt fired by Amick a split second later. He rolled against the back of the couch, looking toward the open door to the suite. Idera was there, filling the room with more energy bolts, alternating between Amick and the last guard. They avoided the bolts, diving for cover among the heavy and opulent furniture in the room.

Rion was caught in the middle of the firefight. He once had an MK, but no longer. That was fortunate. Idera was shooting at anyone with a weapon.

That was until the Lep'sorian launched himself off his strong hind legs and slammed his massive head into Idera. She was thrown back into the corridor with the giant frog hopping after her.

For a moment, Amick and the agent were distracted by Rion and Idera. Adam twisted the chain on the handcuffs and was rewarded when one side broke loose, leaving a ring on one wrist and dangling length of chain on the other. He rose to his feet and jumped, throwing himself back over the sofa and at the table with the detonator.

Amick was a few feet away on his knees, hidden behind an oversized chair with a high back. He saw what Adam was doing and fired off a bolt. It went high, splashing off the enormous picture window along the outer bulkhead.

Adam hit the table hard, expecting to topple it over until he found it was bolted to the floor. His chin bounced off the edge, opening a cut and possibly chipping a couple of teeth. Adam didn't grab the detonator, but he was able to sweep his hand across the surface of the table, clearing it of a lamp, a promotional display and the small electronic device.. It flew to the outer wall under the window.

Amick was next to Adam a second later, planting a powerful kick into Adam's ribs. He didn't get a chance for a second kick before Idera was at the door again and firing in his direction. He had to dive for cover, as he and his last soldier returned fire at the doorway.

But then Idera was hit from behind by Rion's big head a second time sending her tumbling into the room and rolling until she was only a few feet from Adam. She recovered quickly and tossed him an MK.

"You don't obey orders, do you?" Adam scolded as the pair crouched behind the sofa.

"It is one of my strongest attributes. It saves lives."

Adam couldn't argue with that. And then he had a clear shot over Idera's shoulder at Rion coming through the door. He fired the MK, hitting the beast in the chest. The giant frog squealed and then jumped to his right toward the other side of the huge greatroom, leaping a second time for cover behind an entertainment console.

"What is that great ugly beast?" Idera asked. "It seems impervious to flash bolts."

Adam stuck the MK over the top of the sofa and lit off a couple of quick shots.

"That is my client, or what he turned into."

"That skinny, slimy thing became that? I shot it in the hallway with a Xan-fi. It felt it but did not go down."

"I noticed."

"We must run to the door."

"Not without the detonator."

"What detonator?"

"The one on the floor below the window."

Idera looked over, seeing the device. "I will provide cover while you—"

The couch—which had also been bolted to the floor—suddenly toppled over on them, the result of a backward kick from Rion's powerful hind legs. Adam's Human strength, combined with Idera's incredibly strong arms, shoved the couch back over, giving Adam a bead on the last guard. He placed the first bolt in the agent's hip and the second in his back as he fell. But then he found himself under the couch again as Rion bounced on it.

Damn energy bolts, Adam thought. They had no penetrating power, otherwise, Adam would have shot through the fabric and backing of the couch. Instead he crawled along the length and came out the other end. Idera was behind him.

Amick fired two quick bolts at Adam before committing a mortal sin for special operatives: He lost count of his shots. The MK went silent as he lined up on Adam's exposed head. When no bolt was released, he tossed the useless weapon at Adam and jumped.

The pair came together as Amick slapped at the Human's gun hand, knocking it away. As Adam once suspected, Sandon Amick was no Hans Gruber. He was nearly as strong as Adam if a step slower with his reactions. But still, he managed to get a couple of blows to Adam's face before sliding over him and clamping a powerful arm around Adam's neck. The force of the clamp was incredible, making a profound impression on the Human.

Adam pulled on the arm with his hands, which would normally have broken the bones of an alien. But not Amick. He was of a different class, almost the equal of a Human. If Adam lived, he'd have to find out what species Amick was so he could keep an eye out for them. Next, Adam pressed with his feet and slid the combatants along the carpeted floor. Then he rolled over, using his deceptive weight to knock Amick off balance. Now Adam was on top but facing the ceiling, with Amick under him, his powerful forearm still locked around Adam's neck.

In the briefest of moments, Adam wondered where Idera was? He could sure use her timely intervention about now.

Then he heard a Xan-fi go off and another squeal. She had her hands full fending off a crazed giant frog.

Adam threw his head back, hitting Amick with a glancing blow on his cheekbone. He did it again and Amick slid over to his right. Adam next pressed with his legs again, but this time arching his back while twisting, attempting to flip over on top of the alien.

Amick couldn't maintain the grip and let go suddenly, pushing Adam away before crawling on his hands and knees. Adam continued with his flip and he, too, was on his hands and knees. But then he sprung, landing on Amick's back this time.

It was a difficult wrestling match to score, but wrestling had never been Adam's forte. It was boxing.

Amick gained his footing and turned to face Adam. This is where quickness and strength mattered. The fist caught Amick just above his left eye, twisting the bad guy around. However, Adam's blindingly fast left hook stopped his lateral movement, followed by another roundhouse right.

As Amick crumpled to the floor, there wasn't much solid bone left in his skull. There was a possibility he could live after the beating, but he would be a vegetable for the rest of his miserable life.

And then more flash bolts went off behind Adam.

He turned to see a horrifying scene.

Rion was standing on his hind legs, his front legs slapping at the air and his two forearms covering his head. Idera was across the room, firing at the frog. He was hard to miss, but all the shots did were irritate him. His blubbery flesh was red and blistered as it absorbed each flash bolt, but otherwise, it was unbroken.

Idera stopped to load another battery into the weapon.

That's when Rion jumped for the window, using one of his forearms to scoop up the detonator. Then he leaped onto the window and stuck there, using the suckers on his four legs.

"This was not your concern! All you were hired to do was play escort." the Lep'sorian yelled at Adam and Idera. "But now you have sentenced the Borr to another thousand years of near-slavery." With dexterity Adam didn't know he had, Rio flipped open the detonator lid and began to press numbers on the keypad. "Now you will pay the price for your interference...."

Knowing that the damn flash bolts had little effect on the alien, Adam dived for his duffle bag which was only five feet away. The top was open and he slipped his hand inside, knowing where he'd left his MK/Glock-Hybrid. Within the canvas bag, Adam felt the handgrip, expertly flicking the safety off and placing his index finger on the trigger.

He fired with the weapon still in the bag. It didn't matter. An ungodly loud bang sounded in the metal-lined room, sending a round ripping through the fabric and into the flesh of the Lep'sorian. The nine-millimeter, hollow point, one hundred-fifty grain round did have penetrating power, unlike the flash bolts. It tore into Rion's flesh, passing through his blubbery body and striking the thick plate glass of the window. Adam followed the first shot with two more.

And then the window began to spiderweb.

"Run!" Idera screamed as she bolted for the open door.

Adam was two steps behind her when the window burst outward. Rion's body was sucked out, along with the glass, the couch and everything else that wasn't bolted to the floor. Including the detonator.

Idera was through the door just as Adam's hands grasped the door frame.

Then his body was sucked backwards, leaving him suspended in midair in a waterfall of rushing air coming in from the hallway.

The standard door to the suite was still opened inward, but then a thick, emergency pressure door slid out from the frame. Adam's hand still gripped the left side of the portal, while his right clung to the rapidly closing pressure door. The opening was getting narrower and the flow of air stronger.

Adam was about to lose his grip on the pressure door when a vice-like hand clamped onto his left wrist. His right hand slipped off the other side, and he was left dangling in the torrent of escaping air held only by Idera's long, spindly arm.

And then she pulled, and Adam began to move through the rapidly shrinking opening. He managed to get his right arm back up again and used it to make the last final push before the door closed.

He fell hard to the floor, landing on Idera, who coughed and choked as the air was knocked from her lungs. Adam rolled off of her, lifting her head and cradling her to his body.

"Are you all right?" he asked.

"You are heavier than you look," Idera coughed.

"And you're a lot stronger than *you* look."

"In that case, we make a good team."

They laughed, not trying to hide their teeth lest the gesture be misconstrued. Although no one was around to misread the emotion, Adam wouldn't have cared if there were. Because of them, a lot of people would make it off Rizen Station alive.

Chapter 26

The ungrateful Elites were still bitching at Adam's refusal to fly them from Rizen Station when they entered a shuttle that would take them to their waiting ships. Two of their original transports had been destroyed when the MOB-4 blew up, but replacements were sent.

It wasn't hard to locate and defuse the bombs that had been placed aboard, and after that, the air of panic lifted. Adam was a little disappointed that none of the Indies were left to stare with wonder—and jealousy—at he and Idera for what they had just accomplished. No worries, the word would spread, as it always did. *So much for wanting to be anonymous,* Adam thought. Sure, he liked his job—most of the time—but this would only enhance his reputation and bring more work his way.

That was both good and bad.

Tidus would raise the fee for The Human's services, meaning Adam would only go to those with the most credits. That meant assholes like the Elites. He had no desire to work for people like that. He'd have to work something out with Tidus, maybe a sliding scale depending on ability to pay, although that would be a hard sell with the Juirean. Tidus loved his credits.

Even so, the victory on Rizen Station was met with mixed reviews. Yes, all the Delegates and their staff that the terrorists didn't kill had been saved. But the credits were nowhere to be found. The various governments tried to backtrack the deposits, but the galaxy is big and diverse. The original depository only held the funds for a few minutes before they were transferred, which led to another transfer, and then another. Maybe at another time, the trail could have been followed. But not in the chaos that was the present-day Milky Way Galaxy.

Adam and Idera received token congratulations from the owners of the Station and then were sent on their way. On the shuttle to Ladhi, Adam asked Idera what her plans were going forward.

"I do not think I will be welcomed back with San'nor Security. I deserted my team and disobeyed orders."

"And it saved lives," Adam smiled.

"They will not care. Yes, our client lived but my team died."

"Then come to work for Starfire. We could always use another strong arm, and damn, you have a couple of really strong arms."

"Let us keep that a secret. Even San'nor did not know of that. I like to keep some things in reserve. As do you, I can tell." She looked into Adam's strange blue eyes. "You are quite the mystery, Adam Cain. Someday, I will have to research your name."

"Please don't. I left that life behind me. Most of what you'll learn will be stories, fantasies mainly. All I want to do now is fly under the radar—meaning I just want to do my job and not attract too much attention."

"Then, Adam Cain, I would suggest you stop being so *damn* good at your job, to use a Human word. Start by trying to be normal, like the rest of us."

Adam grinned, a wicked, sinister grin while bouncing his eyebrows. "I can try, but what fun would that be?"

Epilogue

Adam was back in the padded chair in Tidus's office, downing his second Diet Pepsi. After what happened during the Juirean's last *simple* job, Adam figured he was owed a whole case of the sweet, carbonated elixir.

"Ninety thousand stinking credits," Tidus was complaining. "Seems like a lot of work for such a measly fee."

"You should see it from my perspective. But you're right. You don't pay me enough for all this crap. Not even close."

Tidus snorted. "You should be glad I paid you anything at all. You know, we received a bill for some of the collateral damage you caused to the station."

"You're kidding!" Adam gasped. "What, did they have trouble getting the blood out of the carpets? Too bad."

Tidus looked at his computer screen. "More than that. A broken window, a lost maintenance jet pack, a broken door to someplace called the Observation Dome, and a broken ventilation fan, along with some other miscellaneous stuff. Damn, that must have been one hell of a big window! They want forty-five grand just for that."

"You're not going to pay it, are you?"

"I have our attorneys on it. They've pointed to the contract where it says, 'collateral damage included.' That means we're not responsible. They were warned. But I'm not worried. If they put up a fight, I'll just send you over to them to negotiate a settlement."

"Very funny. Now, what's next?" Adam asked. "And please, don't make it another *simple* job. I don't think I'd survive another one."

"Well, then, how about a little coup," Tidus announced, punching the keys on his computer. "It's been a while since you took over a planet."

"At least a year. Tell me about it."

"Same old shit; some crazy despot is killing his people and another group wants him gone. A piece of cake. Should take you a week or two."

"We'll see."

"Hey, I'll even let you pick your team."

"Idera?"

Tidus shook his head. "Sorry, she's on another assignment. But you can have anyone else you want. Look through the personnel files and let me know."

For a moment, Adam thought back to Ethan Hunt, looking through the personnel files of the Impossible Mission Force—the IMF—selecting his team.

"So, is this a *Mission: Impossible*?" he asked.

For all his familiarity with Human slang and pop-culture, this one threw Tidus for a loop. "Mission impossible? No way. Don't you know that no mission is *impossible* for the Human for Hire?"

The End

Coming next...

Human For Hire (2)
Soldier of Fortune

Be sure to sign up for the email list to get updates
and notices of the new books coming from T.R. Harris.

And now, a sample from Chapter One in

Human For Hire (2)

Soldier of Fortune

By
T.R. Harris

In a fit of rage, Adam ripped off his helmet. It was useless anyway, having had half of it blown away earlier. He looked around through the blood-tinted sheen at the smoke, fire and devastation wrought by the savage mechanical beasts. The forest was ablaze, ignited by myriad star-hot plasma bolts striking all around, and with the whipping flames herding the survivors toward the sea cliffs a mile away.

Almost the entire assault force of five hundred native liberators had been annihilated. Of Adam's six-person command team, he'd lost two. Tidus wouldn't like that. They were his employees. The native military leader of the now-failed revolution, Wilsom Panasin, only had a handful of his troops still with him and barreling headlong through the forest, just like Adam's mercenaries.

It was not a good day all around.

Indo Saphir, Adam's second-in-command, slipped up beside him.

"The second Spider is down, but the last one is still coming."

"I can hear it," Adam confirmed. "Since when did they start putting horrifying soundtracks in the bastards?"

"It is working to scare our troops even more."

"I know. I'll have to keep that in mind for the next we're in control of the Spiders."

"If there is a next time."

Adam shrugged. There was that consideration.

"We must stop this run," Indo continued. "They intend to chase us over the cliffs."

Adam nodded as he ran. He was much faster than anyone else in the forest, but he moderated his pace so the others could keep up. He also knew his ship was on standby, the seventh member of his team at the controls and awaiting the order to exfil. Seeing a small speeder sweep in and extract the mercenaries wouldn't do much for the morale of the remaining liberators. But what the hell? Their time was short anyway. Nevertheless, Adam was confident he and his people could escape. Not all revolutions were destined to succeed; in fact, very few did.

Even so, Adam was frustrated at the utter failure of his meticulously planned operation. But what was one to expect when you were betrayed? He wasn't a hundred percent sure who it was, but he had a pretty good idea. Dracu Hor, the moneyman/being of the operation, the instigator who had devised the coup originally and then financed it out of his own pocket. Why he would do such a thing was still a mystery. Maybe once Adam had his hands wrapped around the alien's scrawny neck, Dracu would provide some answers. When that might be, Adam wasn't sure. All he knew was that no one doubled-crossed *The Human* and lived to talk about it. At least not for long.

Through the smoke and flames to his rear, Adam saw the forty-foot-tall, six-legged tank/gun turret smash through another grove of trees, spinning the flash cannon barrel to and fro, targeting the fleeing troops. Nicknamed a *Spider*, the mechanical beast was immune to heat and fire and could only be taken out by destroying two of its six spindly legs. Unfortunately, Adam didn't have a lightsaber like Luke Skywalker had when he took on Imperial Walkers. The weapon didn't exist in the real galaxy. The five hundred natives who had begun the assault on the Presidential Compound had Xan-fi rifles, which would have been enough to complete the mission if the Spiders hadn't shown up. But it would take more than flash bolts to take down the monsters.

Adam had equipped his team with ballistic weapons, the latest high-powered weapons imported from Earth. They were rare, not because they weren't effective, but because ammo was almost impossible to find and keep in stock beyond the few worlds that still made up Earth's diminished Orion-Cygnus Union. Adam had to be judicious with their use. That was until they were chased through the native town of Shore's End and into the southern forest. Now, two Spiders had been neutralized, primarily from rounds they took from the modified M88-A assault rifles. But now, their ammo was nearly gone, and there wouldn't be enough to take out the last of the deadly tanks.

"It is almost time to call it," Indo puffed next to Adam. He had at least ten years of experience being an Indie soldier of fortune, and Indo could see the writing on the wall.

That was the thing about mercenaries. They came into the game for the money, but there was no guarantee of success. If the situation became untenable, they would bounce and live to fight another day ... and for another fee.

Not so the poor natives who risked everything at the chance for a better future. Once again, Adam mentally shrugged. Maybe next time.

"All right, make the call," Adam said to Indo.

Relief flooded over Indo's equally bloody and soot-covered face. Originally, his skin was tinged green. Now, it was the uniform black and red of all the other survivors.

"Confirmed," Indo said. The visor on his still-intact helmet was open, allowing Adam and him to talk. Adam's comms had been in his now discarded helmet.

Indo shouted at Adam through the roar of the fire, the flash of energy bolts and the ungodly alien racket that passed for music blaring from speakers in the Spider. "He'll be waiting just below the ledge. We may have to jump."

"Understood.

Just then, Wilsom Panasin sprinted up next to Adam and Indo.

"It had to be Dracu!" he shouted. "He is the only one who knew of our plans."

Wilsom had once been a high-ranking member of President Creel's security guard until it became too much for him to continue. With over a thousand people a day dying in the algae fields, conscripts of the President's sadistic feudal system, the suffering of Wilsom's people became unbearable, and he left, becoming an outlaw and one of the planet's most-wanted fugitives.

All the planet's seven million inhabitants lived on the Australia-sized island of Osino, where the world got its name. None of the population was indigenous to the planet, but after over eight hundred years of colonization, most had earned the right to be called natives.

That was the case with Wilsom. He was as close to a native as they came, and as such, he felt more of a bond with the people than the carpetbagger President, who only immigrated to the world twenty-two years ago. That was when the big push to grow the genetically engineered algae was picking up steam. Used in everything from medicine to makeup across the galaxy, the algae was Osino's only cash crop, and certain powers ensured the green miracle plant kept growing, even at the cost of tens of thousands of lives per year. But that was all to end once the revolution took place.

As with most feudal systems, once the castle was taken, all the surrounding territory would become the subject of the new master. And that new master was to Dracu Hor, with Wilsom as his trusted second. Apparently, Dracu had had a change of mind.

"We're getting off the planet," Adam screamed at Wilsom. "Are you coming with us or not?"

Wilsom stumbled as he ran. Once regaining his traction, angry eyes bore into Adam. "You are abandoning us?"

"It's not our war. We only planned the assault and trained the troops. We weren't counting on a turncoat to screw up everything."

"Define *screw up*; it is not translating."

"Just what you think it means. We were betrayed. It's time to get the hell out of here. You can live and plan another coup, or you could stay here and die."

"That is no choice."

"You're wrong; it's the only choice. But hurry, I see the edge of the cliff right in front of us."

"My troops?"

"We only have room for you. Make up your mind."

Adam's four-person team skidded to a stop only feet from the bluff's edge, overlooking a rocky and wave-beaten shoreline two hundred feet below. Hovering about fifty feet below the top was the team's small transport speeder, the shuttle they used between their main ship and the surface. It was riding on fiery plumes of lifting jets with the top hatch open. Through the front viewport, Adam could see Esnon Yonick motioning with his hands for the team to jump.

"I am unsure," said Indo, looking at the gap, the drop and the dizzying distance to the rocks below.

"You can make it," Adam said. "I'll go first and then help grab the others."

Even so, Adam motioned for Esnon to move a little closer. He did his best, carefully not to clip a stubby wing on the rock outcropping.

Ignoring the indecisive Wilsom, Adam took a casual leap through the air and landed smoothly on the wide metal hull near the hatchway. The jump was a piece of cake for a Human, helped by Adam's superior strength and balance. That was why he went first; the others would need help.

Next came Carpin and Dalin. With each, they landed hard and then slipped, sliding toward the side of the starship before Adam grabbed them and pulled them to safety.

Indo turned to Wilsom. "Your last chance."

The native still hesitated, especially now, looking at the jump he would have to make.

Indo shook his head with impatience ... and jumped.

With his remaining team safely in the shuttle, Adam looked up one last time at Wilsom.

"Your fight isn't over as long as one of you lives on," Adam yelled at the alien.

Adam could see the agony on Wilsom's face. But then it changed to pure terror as he jumped, his arms flailing in the air and a shrill scream coming from his throat.

Adam caught the native without a problem. Wilsom clung to the Human, his knees almost too weak to walk. Indo and Caper helped Wilsom through the hatch.

Adam stood on the hull for a few moments longer, bucking the constant updraft from the sea below and watching the first remnants of Wilsom's army cast themselves over the side of the cliff in their last living act. It was sad and sickening. But there was nothing Adam could do. His job here was done, and not every mission succeeded, even if this was one of the worst losses Adam had ever suffered as an Indie mercenary.

He climbed through the hatch and dogged the door. Esnon was off and headed for the stars when he got the green light on his board.

****

The shuttle was closing on the mid-range starliner Adam had checked out of inventory with Starfire Security to transport him and his crew to Osino over two months before. The mood was somber in the smaller craft, with no one speaking. A loss was a loss, whether in a locker room after a football game or above a planet that was twenty thousand light years from Earth.

"Adam, a link is coming in for you," Esnon reported. "It's from Dracu."

"Dracu...you traitor!" Wilsom cried as he surged toward the pilothouse.

"Back off!" Adam ordered. "I'll handle this."

The bloated, yellow face of the alien/native of Osino smiled at Adam.

"I am glad you survived; I never had a doubt that The Human would make it out of that conflagration."

"So, it *was* you," Adam said acidly. "Why? You could have had it all."

"But I will, Mr. Cain. It seems President Creel heard rumors of a pending coup and approached me with an offer. You are looking at the new Vice-President of Osino, and with Creel promising to step down in a few years to enjoy his ill-gotten gains on a planet more to his liking. As you know, he was not born on Osino, not like Wilsom and me. After some negotiation, it was decided that the revolutionary elements of the population had to be purged and bringing them all to one location to be executed seemed logical."

"And the Spiders?" Adam asked.

Dracu beamed. "I brought them in on my ships. I am quite proud of that insight. They did help in the effort."

"I will kill you, Dracu!" Wilsom yelled from the passenger bay.

Dracu's eyes lit up. "I see our friend Wilsom survived as well. That is too bad. Did you know Creel was grooming him to be his replacement? If only he had waited."

"You're the one who approached Wilsom about staging this little revolution of yours," Adam pointed out. "It wasn't his idea."

"He began the movement when he publicly left the President's service. All I did was take advantage of the growing discontent. Now, I must ask you, what are your intentions going forward? You must know nothing I did was aimed at you personally. I respect your skill and abilities, as does everyone in the galaxy. Hopefully, you will see this as just a job. Your company has been fully paid, so there should be no repercussions."

"That is how it normally goes. We do a service, yet we cannot guarantee results."

"Then there is no animosity between us?"

"I didn't say that," Adam said, his eyes steady and boring into the alien on the screen. "All I'm saying is that I'm a professional, and these things happen now and then. It would be unprofessional to hold a grudge."

"Very good then!" Dracu exclaimed. "I am relieved. It was only business."

"That's right, only business. Even so, I'm going to cut this link now because I can't stand another second of looking at your ugly, traitorous face."

Dracu opened his mouth to speak ... but Adam cut the line before he could get the last word out.

Adam may have appeared calm on the outside, but he was seething on the inside. Yes, it would be unprofessional to hold grudges. But as previously mentioned, no one double-crossed The Human and lived to tell about it, at least not for long. Adam didn't know when or where, but eventually, he would even the score with Dracu Hor.

Wilsom was at Adam's side.

"I wish to enlist your services," he said, his voice deep and serious.

Adam snorted. "You have no credits; in fact, you have nothing. You can't even go back to Osino."

"I realize that, but I want you to kill both President Creel and that traitor Dracu Hor."

"Didn't we just try that?"

"I don't mean a coup—a revolution. I mean an assassination."

Adam laughed. It had been years since he'd been an alien assassin, but he didn't tell Wilsom that. "I'm sorry, that's not what Starfire Security does. We're not assassins."

"But you want to be. I can see it burning in your eyes. Consider it a side job beyond your official duties."

Adam shook his head. "Even if I wanted to, as I said, you have no credits. I may be really pissed at Dracu, but I'm not about to risk my life for nothing."

"Once I am installed as the new President, I will have access to the planetary treasury. I will pay you a million energy credits if you help me. You need not do it alone. I will help. I may not have the skills of The Human, but I am an asset."

Indo and the others were listening, tension on their faces, waiting to hear what Adam would say. A million credits...

Wilsom looked at the others. "And your team can help. I will contribute another half a million for them."

Indo waved his hand and shook his head. "No, thank you. I barely got out of the last mission on Osino with my life. I am not about to go right back in."

The others echoed his sentiment.

Wilsom looked back at Adam. "That will be better. A small team of two. No one will suspect us returning so soon. No elaborate planning or army. Kill them, and let me take it from there. My supporters will rally to my side. They will rejoice in the death of the tyrant and the evil merchant who has been making a fortune off their suffering. I know you want to do it. Say yes, and I will raise the fee to one and a half million."

"Credits you don't have," Adam reiterated.

"If you are successful, I will."

Adam turned to his team.

"Do not look at us," Indo said. "This is entirely your decision. We are going back to Tel'oran. But for a million and a half credits, we would not blame you if you stayed on Osino a little longer."

Adam grinned. Damn, how could he say no? Two quick kills, which in reality would be much simpler than staging a planet-wide coup. He'd done it before, a lot of times. He could almost do it in his sleep. And besides, he owed Dracu Hor a bullet through the head.

"Oh, what the hell," Adam finally said. "It's not like I've never killed an alien before. Besides, these guys deserve it. Okay, Wilsom, you've hired yourself an assassin."

Author Notes

Welcome to the world of **The Human**, one of the last of his kind to still be traveling the space lanes looking for work and causing problems for the alien population.

If you noticed, there's a lot of vague references to **The Human's** background. Well, like everyone, he has a back story. If you're interested in learning more about Adam Cain, you will find a whole series of series featuring him in *The Human Chronicles Saga, The Adam Cain Saga* and *The Human Chronicles Legacy Series*.

The premise of *Human for Hire* is that Humans are the semi-supermen of the galaxy. This has been a consistent theme in all my writing. Seeing that I'm a Human, it's understandable. From the very beginning, I've wanted Humans—that's us—to be proud of our heritage and our special abilities. The problem, we don't know how special we are until we have something else to compare us to. Enter The Aliens, a whole friggin' galaxy of them.

So, if you like feel-good, kick-ass, Human-superiority type of stories, rather than stories about some spore that nearly conquers the Earth—then the *Human for Hire* series is for you.

I'm designing each book so they can be read out of order, so there's no need to start at book one. Pick up any of them and start enjoying the adventures of **Adam Cain: The Human.**

And don't forget to check out all **the 60+ other books I have out,** including the **REV Warriors Series.** Here's another set of books based on the superman principle.

REVs are chemically-enhanced super Marines of the future, the ultimate killing machines, a danger to both friend and foe alike when they're on a drug-induced *Run*.

The series revolves around the first REV who mutates to where he begins producing the REV drug naturally within his own body. This gives him the ability to *activate* at will, something the powers-that-be can't tolerate. If he can activate on his own, that means they can't control him. And what's more dangerous than a superman you can't control?

Anyway, for all my existing fans, I hope you enjoyed ***Human for Hire***. And for all you new fans, welcome. I hope we have a long a fruitful journey together.

T.R. (Tom) Harris
    August 2022

Facebook Group

Also, I'm asking you to join my exclusive, secret,
Super Fan Facebook Group appropriately called

Fans of T.R. Harris and
The Human Chronicles Saga.

*(Which includes fans of **all** my books, but who's being picky.)*
Just click on the link below, and you—yes, **YOU**—may
become a character in one of my books. You may not last long,
and you may end up being the villain, but at least you can
point to your name in one of my books – and live forever!
Maybe. If I decide to use your name. It's at my discretion.

trharrisfb.com

T.R. HARRIS

Email:
bytrharris@hotmail.com
Website:
bytrharris.com

YouTube:
T. R. Harris - The Nomadic Novelist

HUMAN FOR HIRE

Novels by T.R. Harris

Human for Hire Series
Human For Hire
Soldier of Fortune
Devil's Gate
Frontier Justice
Armies of the Sun
Sirius Cargo
Cellblock Orion
Starship Andromeda

The Human Chronicles Legacy Series
Raiders of the Shadow
War of Attrition
Secondary Protocol
Lifeforce
Battle Formation
Allied Command

The Adam Cain Saga
The Dead Worlds
Empires
Battle Plan
Galactic Vortex
Dark Energy
Universal Law
The Formation Code
The Quantum Enigma
Children of the Aris

T.R. HARRIS

<u>The Human Chronicles Saga</u>

The Fringe Worlds
Alien Assassin
The War of Pawns
The Tactics of Revenge
The Legend of Earth
Cain's Crusaders
The Apex Predator
A Galaxy to Conquer
The Masters of War
Prelude to War
The Unreachable Stars
When Earth Reigned Supreme
A Clash of Aliens
Battlelines
The Copernicus Deception
Scorched Earth
Alien Games
The Cain Legacy
The Andromeda Mission
Last Species Standing
Invasion Force
Force of Gravity
Mission Critical
The Lost Universe
The Immortal War
Destroyer of Worlds
Phantoms
Terminus Rising
The Last Aris

<u>The Human Chronicles Box Set Series</u>

Box Set #1 – Books 1-5 in the series
Box Set #2 – Books 6-10 in the series
Box Set #3 – Books 11-15 in the series
Box Set #4 – Books 16-20 in the series
Box Set #5—Books 21-25 in the series

HUMAN FOR HIRE

Box Set #6—Books 26-29 in the series

<u>REV Warriors Series</u>
REV
REV: Renegades
REV: Rebirth
REV: Revolution
REV: Retribution
REV: Revelations
REV: Resolve
REV: Requiem
REV: Rebellion
REV: Resurrection
<u>*REV Warriors Box Set - Books 1-5*</u>

<u>Jason King – Agent to the Stars Series</u>
Jason King and the Unity Stone Affair
Jason King and the Mystery of the Galactic Lights

<u>The Drone Wars Series</u>
Day of the Drone

In collaboration with Co-Author George Wier...
The Liberation Series
Captains Malicious